I0518739

Country boy Johnny's been having a tough time ever since he caught his wife in bed with his best friend and business partner. The comic book café owner and graphic novelist throws himself into his floundering business. He's getting over a nasty divorce and getting on with his life. He can't believe his luck when local vet, Nelson O'Keefe, the only other single guy in town invites him on a trip—a free spa resort vacation he won in an online contest.

For Johnny, whose luck has been down, down, down, things might finally be turning around. Johnny thinks a break is just what he needs, but en route to Montego Bay, he discovers his dream holiday is one big gay Mardi Gras. He freaks. Not only that but he can't get a flight out of St. Maarten for at least a week. Advised by his friends and his traveling companion to have fun and relax, he goes berserk. He's not gay. Never was. Never will be. He's just a country boy. Isn't he?

The unauthorized reproduction or distribution of this copyrighted work is illegal. Criminal copyright infringement, including infringement without monetary gain, is investigated by the FBI and is punishable by up to 5 years in federal prison and a fine of $250,000.

This book is a work of fiction. Names, characters, places, and incidents either are products of the author's imagination or are used fictitiously. Any resemblance to actual events or locales or persons, living or dead, is entirely coincidental.

Country Boy
Copyright © 2019 JC Raefael
ISBN: 978-1-4874-2359-9
Cover art by Martine Jardin

All rights reserved. Except for use in any review, the reproduction or utilization of this work in whole or in part in any form by any electronic, mechanical or other means, now known or hereafter invented, is forbidden without the written permission of the publisher.

Published by eXtasy Books Inc or
Devine Destinies, an imprint of eXtasy Books Inc

Look for us online at:
www.eXtasybooks.com or www.devinedestinies.com

Country Boy
Country Boy Book 2

By

JC Raefael

DEDICATION

To Nathan and Ruth, with love.

CHAPTER ONE

Not much can get me out of bed most mornings, and a frosty fall day is my idea of the perfect time to stay under the covers and listen to the radio. Something . . . some inner sixth sense woke me that day and forever changed my life . . .

I didn't hear any noise, though I was aware of activity outside. A scrawny coyote had lurked for two years in the patchy garden of my sprawling, dilapidated ranch house in Meiners Oaks, a blink of an eye south of Ojai. I assumed it was him and paid him no mind as I listened to the Lady Antebellum song, 'Need You Now.' I adore that song and long to love and need somebody like that.

For a moment, I thought about the coyote. He'd realized I was harmless, and sought refuge from the searing valley heat in my garden most nights and early in the morning. I guess we both appreciated living in one of the last cowboy and orange grove towns in southern California.

It wasn't unusual for a wild creature to be seeking refuge here. Most of us knew the rangy critter, who'd showed up as a pup a couple of years before in this soothing pocket of eucalyptus-infused oasis. Located just an hour and a half north of the madness of Los Angeles and half an hour south and slightly inland from the hoity-toity beach community of Santa Barbara, Meiners Oaks, to me, was paradise.

This hardy coyote, like me, had found its sweet spot. We kinda liked each other. I didn't feed him and he didn't try to eat my cat. I had just the one, a big Maine Coon called Pablo.

I would have been damned pissed if the coyote munched on my pal. Instead, he fed on rodents and scraps that mysteriously showed up in various places on my property on Ash Lane. He ate, and I turned a blind eye to his sleeping arrangements in the old dog den on the back of my property.

Occasionally, well, okay, often, I gave him water in a big steel bowl I kept on the back porch. He was a skinny guy, but like I said, he was hardy.

When I awoke a little after six, I got up and trotted to the kitchen, looking out the window. He was lying in the grass. He lifted his head when he sensed me. He was too skinny to be handsome, but he kinda was. There was a nobility to him. He dropped his head again and licked his paws. I brewed me some Starbucks Christmas blend and contemplated toast or an English muffin. When I heard the crackle of gunfire, it surprised me.

The agonized yelp that followed had me running out the back door, Pablo close on my heels. I shut the cat indoors, feeling his fury prickling at the back of my neck. The coyote lay in a bloody heap right where I'd just spotted him in the middle of the garden. His pain-filled eyes looked up at me. Half his body tried to move, while the other half lay paralyzed. He'd been shot in the back. The poor guy whined again. Geez, who the hell could have taken a potshot at a perfectly good pest controller?

I scanned the property line. Movement at the far corner on the other side of the fence told me somebody still lurked.

"Leave him alone," I commanded. "He isn't bothering anyone."

Whoever had targeted the coyote remained where he was. I was pretty certain it was a he. I could hear heavy breathing.

"Earl? Is that you?"

Silence except for the scary breathing, both from the coyote and the gun-crazy asshole on the other side of the fence.

"You okay, Johnny?" my neighbor Billy asked over our adjoining fence. He poked his head over the newly-painted line of redwood.

"Call 911. Somebody just shot the coyote."

Billy's face turned grim. I'd pretended not to know it was Billy who fed the coyote. I heard him on his cell phone. The coyote lay still. I approached him. His breathing was shallow, his tongue lolling out of his open mouth. His eyes were open, his expression glassy.

By the time the police arrived, the coyote was in acute agony and I was damned upset. I kept my hand on his flank. His fur felt wiry to the touch. He'd allowed me to pet him once in all the time I knew him, but he was my pal. I stole a look over my shoulder and glimpsed Pablo's little ears in the kitchen window, his head erect at an odd angle. This was the way he usually held it when the coyote came near.

The cops in Meiners Oaks are a friendly bunch, and one of them called the local vet. I hardly knew Nelson O'Keefe since Pablo was a healthy cat, but Nelson, dressed in pajama bottoms and a thick, nobbly sweater that looked homemade, greeted me and knelt beside me. He began preparing an injection.

"I'm going to put him out of his misery, Johnny," he said. "It's the kindest thing we can do for him."

"No," I said. "Can't you save him?"

"His spine is shattered. He's paralyzed."

The coyote was close to death, I was certain, but I still wanted to fight for him.

"I have money, I'll pay for it."

Nelson looked up at me, shaking his head. "Johnny, he's badly injured."

I took a deep breath and watched him tape up the coyote's paw. He administered a sedative and the dog's rapid, agonized breathing slowed.

"Good boy," I said, stroking the coyote's thigh, when Nelson injected the final, pink stuff. And just like that, the coyote was gone.

Nelson hung out with me and the dead furry guy, but the cops cleared out. I wanted to bury the coyote on my property, but Nelson said it was against the law.

"Can't we bend the rules just once?" Billy asked, coming over with a shovel.

"I can pretend I know nothing." Nelson shrugged. "I'm kinda good at that."

We buried the coyote near the dog house, and except for the massive amount of blood where he'd been shot, he might never have been there at all.

It hit me hard. Harder than maybe it should have, but coyotes have a right to live as much as anybody else. I tried not to look at it as another loss.

Nelson was awesome. I knew he ran the local vet hospital with his aging father, and that his mom was their front office person. I also knew that people requested Nelson to tender their pets because he had a way with animals. His old man, on the other hand, tended to be grumpy and loved to tell people to declaw their indoor cats.

Nelson hosed off the blood, and I offered him and Billy coffee. We sat on the porch like three old men, staring out at the eucalyptus trees, mugs in hand, swinging on the rocking chairs I'd picked up dirt cheap at Treasures of Ojai antique mart. And we weren't old. Not me and Nelson, anyway. He had a thatch of dark, unruly hair and bright blue eyes. He smiled a lot.

Like me, he was in his early thirties, and I knew he had a girlfriend. She had been the vet tech in his hospital. I wondered how it was going. I, too, had dark hair, as well as a persistent shadow of a beard that appeared within an hour of my morning shave. I had eyes the color of dirt. At least, that's what my ex-wife said. I sipped my Starbucks and tried not to feel bitter about Sam. She'd always hated the comic book store and café I owned and managed on Ojai Avenue up in Ojai, but liked some things about it. She ran off with my business partner. Yeah, Frankie was a total bastard. Stole my wife, stole my Ford SUV and emptied our business bank accounts. Yay him.

I wondered how he was getting along with Sam, whose favorite pastime, apart from shopping, was complaining.

"How ya doing these days?" Billy asked as we swung in companionable silence.

I knew he was referring to Sam.

"Okay, I guess."

Billy was a cool guy. The coolest. He fed all the local stray cats, and he'd kept his eye on the coyote. At the age of sixty-six he'd retired, and he and his wife lived on a comfortable income. They worked every day in one local charitable organization or another, donating their time and their money. I deeply respected him.

"You missing her any?"

"No," I said, and it was true. We'd been married five years. She'd been gone six months, and each day, the pain lessened. I eased it some by keeping busy, and now I had a new line of comic books, or rather, graphic novels I'd started with my buddy, Ellis, who lived in New York. We published one a month, and we were up to number twelve in our series of boy gangster stories. They were doing well. The comic book store . . . not so much.

Ellis and I worked via email. I wrote the stories, and he was the artist. I hadn't seen him for six years, since he'd moved back east with his college professor wife, Genevieve. He had come up with the idea for *Gangsta Guys*. His idea was to use it as a platform for his wonderful artwork.

I jumped at the chance to write the tales because the money we made was pretty good and I could work from home. My theory was, I could churn out the novels and one day get to my Great American Novel lurking in my bottom drawer. Only I never did.

"Has something happened?" Nelson asked. "Who's gone?"

"His wife left him." Billy drained his coffee. "Got any more of this mud?"

I didn't take offense. Billy called coffee mud. He liked his coffee strong, just like me.

"Help yourself," I told him, and he let himself inside. I could hear him having a long conversation with Pablo, promising him chicken leftovers, and I felt Nelson's touch on my hand.

"Man, I had no idea. How long has it been?"

"Six months."

"Wait . . . did she and Frankie—"

"Yep," I said, cutting him off. I could deal with her betrayal if I didn't have to think or talk about it. Talking about it kinda opened up the half-healed wounds. The sensation wasn't so much fun.

"I heard something about that. Only, I heard he took your most expensive comic books and your money."

"Yeah," I said. Very few people knew that I cared more about him stealing my wife than the comic books.

"You got cleaned out," he said.

"Guess I did."

"I'm sorry about the coyote. Any idea who shot him?"

"My guess is it mighta been Earl."

Earl was the neighborhood curmudgeon. He'd been waiting seventy-two years for a break-in that had never happened. He once shot a meter reader, mistaking him for a burglar. He sat in perpetual vigil with a 38 on his lap and an American flag dangling from his front door. Sometimes, when Earl was itching to get into some trouble, he made it happen.

"He's such a tool," Nelson said, which just about wrapped up my ideas on the subject.

We finished our coffees and bid each other a last farewell. Billy was off to the run the inter-faith soup kitchen at the Krotona Institute, and Nelson joked about having a hot date with a string of surgeries. He was a cool vet. On Wednesdays, he spayed and neutered all the cats and dogs that the local shelter had. I knew this because when I got Pablo, the shelter gave me a certificate to take to Nelson's vet hospital.

And so, we went about our days. I'd wrecked my diligent two-hour window for my early-morning writing routine before heading to the store. I had about twenty minutes left, so I had to make the most of it. I sat at my desktop computer working on a new science fiction tale Ellis and I were doing. The *Gangsta Guys* had stolen the wrong car and ended up in space in this latest installment of the saga.

Sometimes Ellis came up with these wild ideas, sometimes I did. Mine however, came of a genuine urge to leave this goddamn planet. I'm not sure about Ellis, but I suspect pot might be involved in some of his crazier creations.

I couldn't think, which meant I couldn't write. I was more upset by the coyote being gone than I cared to admit.

It felt weird to know I'd never see his haunting eyes again. He'd been so happy, lying in the grass, licking his paws just a couple of hours ago. I thanked God I never let Pablo out of the house. I wouldn't have to worry about Earl taking a shot at him. Now I saw a squirrel darting across the yard, as if checking the coast was clear. The coyote had kept all the neighborhood wildlife at bay. Now here they were; a new hierarchy forming. No respect!

I swiveled in my chair, trying to dredge up the lightness of being required to write my graphic novels. I couldn't. I drifted online, checking eBay for new comic books for the store. That thieving bastard, Frankie, had hand-picked my best selections and done who knew what with them. He'd really left me in the soup. In all the months since he and Sam had left town, I kept finding other people he'd screwed over. His landlord, his own wife and, apparently, a few of our comic book customers who'd brought valuable comics over on consignment.

Two had threatened to sue when I could find no trace of their comics. All of them had invoices typed up by Frankie on our company letterhead, so I knew they weren't lying, but I had no idea what he'd done with their stuff. I didn't want a trail of lawsuits behind me. Divorce was painful enough. I paid each of the betrayed sellers fair market prices for their comics. I had just finished paying off the last special consignment guy and could now afford to pick up a few well-priced graphic novels and comic books for the store.

It was no use. My mind kept tossing me back to the coyote's side.

I shut the computer down, too agitated to do anything but head to work. I checked Pablo's dishes, ignored what I called his hooded look, and locked up the house.

They say that every house in Meiners Oaks is situated under a live oak tree and it's true. The one shading mine was like action central, with squirrels scurrying from its sprawling branches to my roof. Next stop, my garden. Word must have spread that the coyote was gone. If you've never heard a squirrel chattering, it sounds almost bird-like. I could almost hear them squealing, *Ding dong the witch is dead!*

My Ash Lane house bordered a big stretch of unoccupied land on three sides, the fourth abutting Billy's property. Built in the 1940s by an architect with a taste for Spanish archways and fireplaces in every room, my home was my sanctuary, At least it had been until that morning. I was grateful to have Billy for a neighbor and not loony Earl.

I drove along El Roblar, the main drag, and noticed the cops parked outside Earl's house. Probably they, too, had suspected him of being the culprit. I wondered if he'd be arrested, or even if he'd tried squeezing off a few shots as they strolled through his front gate. Earl wasn't fussy who he shot, as long as he hit a moving target.

The drive into Ojai itself took just a few minutes. The Mariposa Highway also intrigued me. Antique stores stocked over-priced furniture on the sidewalks, hoping to snare witless tourists. Arnaz Farms had foolishly sold off their barn to people peddling supposed country jams and cozy knick-knacks. Maybe they were country but they sure weren't the farm-fresh apples and peaches of my youth.

I'd grown up in Ojai and I'd traveled the country a bit, but marriage had tamed me. I'd opened my business in my twenties with Frankie. In those days, we had it in Santa Barbara, but Sam wanted to move back to Ojai because she wanted a horse. Lots of people owned horses in Ojai. So, we moved back and opened the store. I bought her a horse, which, it turned out, was about the most expensive hobby you could have, except for car racing.

When she and Frankie ran off, she even took the horse. I wondered about him from time to time. At least she left me Pablo.

On East Ojai Avenue, I experienced a sense of calm at the rolling green hills and slopes at the foot of the Topa Topa Mountains. Horses grazed in pristine schoolyards. As a kid in school, we each got our own horse to care for. It taught us responsibility they said. Hence, my desire to have a clean financial slate.

Most businesses were clustered on East Ojai Avenue. Just about my favorite was the O-hi Frosty Freeze. I stopped by every afternoon for a cone. There is no truth to the rumor that I've shoved little kids out of the way to get my ice cream. No siree, not me.

The gateway to the main drag of Ojai never failed to charm me with its converted stables now housing boutique stores, cafés and art galleries. The post office with its clock tower exemplified Spanish architecture at its best. I got parking on Matilija Street, off the main drag, and sat for a moment. I constantly thanked my lucky stars that my business, while not exactly thriving, remained open. So many wonderful places had closed in the last couple of years thanks to the economic recession. We prayed for weekends when tourists thundered into town, but sometimes those two days couldn't make up for the other five days' of drifting foot traffic.

I'd seen my friends suffer and struggle. Some had left town. Some had taken day jobs in other existing businesses. Me, I was just glad I'd been able to get a new alarm system in case Frankie got any smart ideas about coming by to finish the job he started, cleaning me out.

The Comic Café was my pride and joy. I had an old-fashioned soda fountain counter with red pleather-topped stools. I sold coffee, tea, hot chocolate, and cold drinks. My comic books, however, dominated the joint. When Sam was still with me, she made pretty cool sandwiches. Now I bought stuff from the health food store down the road. I thought they were *blech*, but my customers weren't fussy, because they were cheap. Besides, since the food quality had deteriorated I had fewer comic book casualties. I'd lost tons of 'em due to people reading them at the counter and the two tables I'd put in by the windows. People thought nothing of messing up their condition. Mayo, coffee, jam . . . you name it, glued the pages together and made them impossible to sell. With crappy food came brisker business, so as far as I was concerned, that part was good.

I opened up the store, got the coffeemaker going, and two teenagers who should have been in school bounded in.

"You got the new *Spider-Gwen#1*?" one of them asked.

He was in luck. I'd received a new shipment the night before and had even taken time to unwrap the delivery pallets before I went home. I'd expected good sales on the first comic book focusing on the breakout female star of the *Spider-Man* series, but not this early in the day. The kids each snapped up a copy and moved over to the vintage comic section.

"Wow! Cool!" One of them shouted, picking up *Astonishing X Men*. Not exactly vintage, but I'd priced it to sell.

The shorter of the two kids was a *Batman* guy, only he liked the original, not the new artwork. He'd picked up a copy of the graphic novel *Batman: Venom* here for a good price and he always checked for that rare find all Batman fans yearned for: *Detective Comics* Number 27, featuring Batman before he was famous. The street value was over a million dollars. One had just sold at auction for a million three-eighty. You can bet your life it wouldn't be sitting in my store. It would be sold by me and I'd be on my private island in Barbados writing full time.

The kids rifled through the vacuum-sealed offerings, paid for their comics, and went off to bug the lady next door. The Waffle Exchange was exactly what the name implies. It was a serious breakfast place that served up mouth-watering stuff all day long. This being Ojai, however, most businesses closed at five. I stayed open an extra hour to try and catch lingering pedestrians, especially on weekends.

We got a huge amount of business on those days thanks to day trippers. Public holidays were a goldmine, and I usually hired part-time help those days. Since Sam's defection, I'd had qualms about the quality of my health-nut sandwiches and keeping an eye on kids' sticky fingers in my comic book stacks, but I'd survived.

I finished unpacking my shipment and even found a pretty decent ten-year old *Batman* comic my teenaged customer would love. I thought about keeping it behind the counter for his next visit, but stuck it in the stacks along with all the others. Let him think he'd found a bargain. Everyone loved one of those.

My morning was busy, and I was surprised to have made six sales on a Wednesday, which was typically my slowest day. My own personal hump day. A lull in customers allowed me to fire up the new shop desktop computer and I checked my online comic bids.

A guy I'd never seen before strolled in and began going through the new graphic novels.

"You know, these are much cheaper on Amazon," he said.

Here we go.

"No, they're competitively priced," I said. I had this discussion on a daily basis. Amazon. Goddamned Amazon had killed brick and mortar businesses.

The guy held up a new Action Comic graphic novel. "I saw this online five dollars cheaper."

I shrugged. "Really? I priced it at the exact same price . . . and don't forget on Amazon you're paying for shipping as well."

Take that, Internet hijackers!

The guy tried to beat the price down but I declined. I'm not a Turkish bazaar and I wasn't desperate. The book would sell.

He muttered, "Asshole," and walked out the door.

"Have a nice day," I said. *You're the asshole.*

The shop phone rang. It was my friend and writing partner Ellis.

"How's it hangin'?" he asked. Only Ellis could get me smiling at such teenage jokes.

I sighed. "I'm trying to remember my secret code to get

into the shop computer."

"You forgot it again?"

I'd had to set up a complicated system of passwords, thanks to Frankie and Sam messing with the computer and deleting two years' worth of customer records and my entire Quickbooks accounting system. Thanks to my neighbor Billy's eleven-year old grandson's nimble computer skills, most of it had been retrieved. The kid had also helped me set up password-protected features, but I'd be damned if I could remember any of it.

"Hang on," Ellis said. "You emailed it to me, remember?"

"Yeah. But I can't get into the 'puter to check my email."

"Ah, but I've got it right here." He read off some numbers and, hey, presto, open sesame and all that good jazz, I was in.

"Thanks, bro."

"No problemo. How are ya, guy?"

"I'm fine, thanks. I'm lovin' the outer-space storyline."

He chuckled. "I'm thinking a pirate galleon and a sampan with evil sea traders for the next one."

"Why not?"

The teenaged *Batman* fans were back. I saw them move straight over to the stacks and I smiled to myself. I'd priced the book well, just for him. I tuned back into my conversation with Ellis. He would often come up with ideas and pitch them to me over the phone. If I went crazy over them, he'd email me illustrations. He kept me busy, that's for sure. We talked a minute longer and then he had to go. His wife wanted to have sex.

Some days, I wanted to hate Ellis, the lucky, ducky, fucky bastard.

I had a look around the store. The two kids were gone. I was surprised they hadn't mentioned the comic book. I thought they'd go nuts. Some instinct made me go over and

I rifled through the stack. *Gone.* The fucking book was gone. They'd stolen it!

Calm down. Check again.

My heart raced, my palms sweating as I leafed through each plastic casing. Nope. No doubt about it. Man . . . this sucked.

My hopeful spirits sank faster than day-old donuts. Why would they do this to me? I'd been more than generous with these kids. First the coyote. Now this. Bad stuff happened in threes, didn't it? I braced myself for some other piece of fucked-upness to come my way. I even walked to the shop windows to make sure some drunk driver wasn't heading my way to plow into the building.

Turning away again, I didn't see him coming in, but I heard his voice.

"Hey, Johnny."

I turned back. Nelson was wearing hospital garb. Right. Surgery day.

"How you doin'?" I asked.

"Listen . . . you're the first person I thought of. I just won the trip of a lifetime to sunny, sandy, sexy Saba."

"Saba?" I gaped at him.

"Yeah. Saba Island."

"Um. I've never heard of it."

He shrugged. "I'd never heard of it either. It's a small Caribbean island. I checked it out online and it's beautiful. I just won a trip for two to some new resort there." He looked so happy. "I've been trying to win radio contests for two years now. I enter everything on that classic music station. This is the first time I won anything. Except tickets to a music festival that got cancelled, so that doesn't count.

"Well, that's cool."

"You're the only other single guy I know. Apart from Earl, and I sure as shit do not want to travel with *him*. I asked a couple of my friends and they can't come. You wanna come with?"

I blinked. "To Saba?"

He nodded, looking ecstatic.

"When?"

"We'd leave Saturday, for a whole week."

I didn't know what to say. I was depressed as heck. I hadn't had a vacation in two years, I'd worked my way through a huge life upheaval and now somebody had just stolen one of my comics. Saba might be the inspiration I needed for my own work. I was sorely in need of a bit of sun, sand . . . hell . . . maybe even some sex!

"Aren't you in a relationship?" I asked.

He shook his head. "That ended badly."

"Oh. I'm sorry to hear that. I didn't know."

He waved his hand. "No reason you would. So, how about it?"

"How much?" I asked. I was so afraid of the answer but I had to know, obviously. "How much would it cost?"

He smiled. "It's free. We just pay for transportation to the airport and food once we get there."

Sensing my inclination to jump in with both feet and a pair of flippers, he added, "It's an incredible new eco-friendly resort in Well's Bay, which is apparently the best beach on the island. They provide all the transportation from the minute we get to LAX to our arrival in Philipsburg. We fly into St. Maarten and from there take a ferry to Saba."

"Saba!" *Say-ba.* I practiced the word and it felt good on my lips. I warmed up to the idea. Didn't Ellis want to add an oceanic storyline to our next collaboration?

Nelson and I tossed the idea around a bit. We'd drive to LA together. It'd take us an hour and a half. We'd park in long-term parking and take the shuttle to the American Airlines terminal.

Nelson explained that the flight included a stop in Miami, Florida, where we'd spend the night Saturday. We'd fly out Sunday for the three-hour hop over to St. Maarten, then take the five p.m. ferry to Saba Island.

"We don't arrive there until close to eight o'clock at night, but I'm sure we'll find plenty to do. We can rest up and start early Monday with our sight-seeing and hiking."

It sounded great to me. As we discussed the details, I sympathized with Nelson's quest for a suitable traveling companion. Most guys in our town were married or living with their girlfriends. It was weird to invite them on a tropical vacation when they'd obviously want to go with their partners. I couldn't think of too many reasons to pass up a free week-long vacation and I said yes.

"Sounds like a great idea to me, Nelson. I'm wow . . . I'm gonna need some sunblock!"

"Cool," he said, looking relieved.

I found myself grinning and nodding and mentally began packing my bags.

My phone rang. "What about your work?" Ellis asked as soon as I took the call. Trust Ellis to try and poke holes in my flimsy plans.

"I'm going to buy a laptop," I announced. Man, he'd only been suggesting it for months now.

Ellis suddenly liked the idea. We went over the idea of how I'd get my hands on one in time for the trip just three days away. I needed to work through Friday since I'd be closing the store for the next eight days.

"Why do you need to do that?" Ellis asked. "Can't you get your part-timers to keep it open?"

"I don't trust *anyone* anymore. Except you and Billy. You guys are my best friends and I'm about to put the bite on him to feed Pablo for me while I'm away." I sighed. "I got a comic book stolen this morning. I know it's silly but it kinda . . . broke my heart."

"It's not silly. Not after what you've been through." His voice was gruff. Ellis was such a great guy.

"You know what?" he said, "I'm gonna come out there. I've been wanting to come and check out the joint. I'll fly out tomorrow and you can show me the ropes all day Friday. I'll stay at the house and I'll feed that baby mountain lion of yours."

I felt a lump forming in my throat. "You'd . . . you'd do that for me?"

Ellis had wanted to come out when Sam left me and my life was in pieces but I'd begged him not to. His wife, Genevieve, had been going through chemo. A divorce was a snip in comparison. Now, she was in remission and back at work.

"I can't wait," he said, sounding enthusiastic about his own suggestion. Gen's got a friend staying for a couple of weeks." His voice dropped. "To be honest, I can't stand the woman. This is like a dream come true." He paused. "Hey, you know what, get online and check out the new Apple laptops. Find something you like and I'll drop by the Apple Store and pick it up for you."

We tossed that ball around for a minute or two. I went online and found one I liked, and with a slight moment of financial panic, committed myself to the purchase of a thirteen inch Macbook Pro. Yikes. I took a deep, calming breath when I remembered the lovely words, *tax write off.*

I thought about Googling Saba Island, but then a call came in and I got distracted. I had a lot to do before I left, including putting together a list of instructions for Ellis. I sailed through the next twenty-four hours until he arrived. Even Pablo thought the trip was a swell idea. He took the appearance of my suitcase on the bedroom floor as his new personal cocktail lounge and only detested the idea of my upcoming trip when my clothes and shoes found their way into his new club house.

Shopping for a few summery clothes seemed like a good idea. I closed the store for an hour the following morning and ran over to the thrift store on Montgomery. Some guy with a penchant for Bermuda shorts and Hawaiian shirts had donated a bunch of stuff that looked new. I bought it all, raced home, tossed everything in the washing machine, then checked on Pablo. He was asleep on his back in the suitcase, his tummy begging for a rub. I rubbed it. He opened his eyes and stared at me in a glazed way, then closed them again. It's a tough life, having your naps interrupted.

Billy thought the trip was a fine idea and said to let Ellis know he'd be around to help out with Pablo. I couldn't think of anyone else who needed to know my travel plans, and it was only then it dawned on me. All my friends, except for Ellis and Billy were gone. Had they all taken Sam's side? I thought about whom I missed the most, but didn't have much time to ponder the mysteriousness of my empty friend nest. I close the store a little early and made the drive into LA to pick up Ellis from Burbank's Bob Hope Airport, which was forty-five minutes closer to me than LAX. He'd managed to snag a really good deal on Jet Blue.

It was great to see him. He looked damned good. His dark hair had tiny strands of silver through it, which only gave him a more distinguished look. He was waiting outside the small terminal as we'd arranged, and he dumped my Apple Store bag, his suitcase and laptop in the back seat.

He'd always favored jeans and sweaters, and I was pleased to see nothing had changed.

"I have my heart set on Boccali's crab pizza," he said by way of a greeting.

That made me laugh. I loved Boccali's, too. However, since it was back in Ojai, we had to wait a little over an hour to get our hands on the best pizza in the world.

For the entire drive, he vented about Genevieve's visiting friend. He felt left out, I think, judging by his derogatory comments. He claimed that Gen hardly noticed he was leaving, which I doubted. Theirs was the most solid relationship I knew, second only to Billy's and his wife Jude's.

I could allow Ellis the space to whine. He'd sure given me plenty from the moment I found Sam in our bed with Frankie. Yeah, that was a trip and a half to the mental ward in my mind. I'd gone home to pick up some comic books I'd left by mistake, and caught them going at it. A few of my friends asked how I could stay in the house after an incident like that. Easy. It was my salvation. I didn't blame the house for her infidelity. I blamed the two people involved. Even now, I could visualize his pimply white, hairy ass over her prone body.

She took the bed with her, thank God. And Frankie, too. I'd been too embarrassed to say anything when I caught them. She'd looked up, seen me, then smiled. *Smiled.* I still wondered how long she'd hated me and *why* she'd hated me so much.

Back in Ojai, Ellis and I demolished pizza and some perfect, frosty micro brewed Fat Tires, and our conversation turned to me. Me, the comic book geek, whose luck had been down, down, down.

"I think things might finally be turning around for you," he said. We toasted my trip, our fabulous collaboration, and he leaned in to me.

"Take some condoms. Take a big box. I checked out your Saba Island online. It looks amazing. They say it's the most tolerant island in the Caribbean. I must tell my brother. Same sex couples are even allowed to marry there."

I grinned at him. Ellis's brother, Edward, had been having about as much luck with men as I had with women.

Ellis patted my hand and grabbed the check. "You meet a

coupla hot chicks, you're gonna need more than a few love gloves. Better safe than sorry."

For the first time in months, I laughed. A real, honest-to-God belly laugh. It felt damned good.

CHAPTER TWO

M y good humor held up over the next couple of days. It wasn't until I was on the flight to Miami with Nelson that we had a lengthy conversation. We'd talked in snatches the day before. He'd come to the store and met Ellis, who fit right in to my geeky world. The night before I left, Nelson performed an emergency surgery on a golden retriever that had eaten twelve rolls of quarters.

"He's now on a coin-free diet," he said with a cheerful grin before going off to have dinner with his parents and temporary replacement vet.

"Nelson seems like a nice guy," Ellis said as we had dinner at the excellent Exotic Thai restaurant, right across the road from the store. Ellis swooned over the green curry.

"It's as good as I remembered," he said.

Back home, he'd helped me set up my new laptop, and it sat snug in its travel bag at my feet. I was keen to get online since the captain had announced there was WiFi available for those who wanted it. I was dying to send Ellis an email from midair. I thought he'd get a kick out of it.

There were three problems with my scheme, however. One, the guy in front of me was so close it made opening my tray table difficult as it was, let alone with a laptop perched on it. The second problem was that Nelson was in a talkative mood.

The third was the nature of his revelations.

"Since my boyfriend and I broke up . . ." was how it

began.

"Boyfriend?"

He glanced at me, looking shocked. "What ... you didn't ... I mean, you really didn't know I was gay?"

I swallowed and shook my head. I had no problem with gay people, in theory. In fact, I had a gay friend in Ojai. But since my divorce, Joe had vanished like so many others.

"But I thought you were dating one of your vet techs," I said.

"Yeah, I was. Joe. He was a good friend of your wife's."

Oh, so that explained Joe's defection.

Nelson shifted in his seat and stared at me.

"I don't understand something. You seem really stunned to learn I'm gay, but Sam told everyone she left you because you're gay."

"She ... *what?*"

He was the one who looked surprised now.

"She was cheating on *me*," I said, "with Frankie."

"Yeah, but she said you were gay. She said her affair happened because you wanted ... well ... you know ... guys."

I had a bad feeling now about this trip.

"Nelson ... this resort we're going to, is it, um ... gay?"

He lifted his shoulders. "Sure it is."

Oh, shit! No wonder he couldn't get any of his friends interested in going. They all had *girl*friends.

I began to panic. What the hell was I going to do? I couldn't spend a week in an all-gay resort. *Oh man, my bad luck is following me! Me and my super-duper big box of condoms.*

"Didn't you Google Saba?" he asked. "It's the only GLBT-friendly island in the Caribbean."

"No, but Ellis did. He mentioned it. His brother is gay and he thought he'd be interested in going. " I felt miserable. I had no problem with gay people, except that I'd hoped to bed at least one woman.

"Would you prefer to fly home once we reach Miami?" he

asked, his tone tight.

"Of course not."

Silence for a moment. "You're worried you won't meet any straight women," he said.

Wow, he was positively psychic.

"Yeah."

"Well, I can't say for sure, but since it's so gay-friendly and the resort is new, maybe there'll be some straight, lonely women there. Most gay men I know adore their women friends. I'll bet there are plenty of them going since it's supposed to be a hot new place. It won't all be love-up dudes."

I brightened. "You think so?"

"Sure. And don't forget, it's really an untouched piece of paradise in comparison with other places in the islands. We're staying at the Blue Hills Resort and it's gay and lesbian-oriented, but I promise you won't feel uncomfortable."

"How do you know? Have you been there?"

"No. But Sabans are very laid-back people and this place is supposed to be filled with natural charm and a lot of outdoor activities. It's not like a West Hollywood meat market."

I started to relax. He was right. I had to be positive. Maybe it would be okay.

"You know what?" he said, touching my arm. "You'll still have a good time. Saba is supposed to be a fantastic place with tons to do. It's called the Unspoiled Queen of the Caribbean."

Queen. Oh. My. God.

He must have seen my expression. "Not that kind of queen. The regal kind. Don't worry," he said. "In my experience, gay men don't run after straights. You might meet some women at some of the hotels nearby. There are a few really nice ones. Hey, we'll have dinner out, we can take a hike. I'm looking forward to trying out the bamboo river rafting—"

River rafting. That sounded nice and macho. Unless the guys were all nude and bamboo was code for clutching one another's cocks. I felt the panic rising again.

Focus on the positive.

Girls. Hotels. Yeah. I nodded, trying not to picture myself popping open an emergency exit, grabbing a couple of beers and hurling myself off the plane like that crazy Jet Blue flight attendant.

Nelson sipped his soda and slid his iPod earphones into his ears. His gaze shifted to the screen just above us. He had a big ol' smile on his face. The movie *Dinner For Schmucks* was just starting. Yeah, easy for him to sit back and have a chuckle. I was in torment! I was on a trip for schmucks! *Jet Blew!*

Oh. My. God.

With Nelson distracted, I quit dithering. I capped the bottled water on my tray table and put it in the seat pocket. I grabbed my laptop and fired it up, then sent Ellis an email.

Help. Nelson is gay. The trip is gay. A gay resort! What am I going to do?

I waited a couple of seconds, hoping he'd respond. I made sure Nelson was watching the movie. I liked the guy, but I was floundering. My wife had told people I was gay! She'd made me the bad guy. I sent a second email and was stunned when Ellis wrote back.

Hey, you'll be in Saba. Smoke tons of ganja. You never know. You might meet a guy you like.

A howl of laughter beside me let me know Nelson wasn't watching the movie anymore. I stole a glance in his direction. Oh, yeah. He was reading the email.

Ellis responded to my second email about Sam telling everyone I was gay.

Gen and I had a bet. I told her it wasn't true. Guess I win ten bucks.

Boy was I mad! Sam had even told Ellis and his wife, and

Gen believed it. I felt a bit better that Ellis put money on my sexuality. What a great friend he was —

A third email popped up.

You've got condoms. Make the most of them.

Nelson laughed, but I was mortified. My best friend was a total ass.

I went online and typed in Saba. It had an active volcano.

All right. Don't panic. The photos were gorgeous. The official website for the island stated: *You'll find no franchises here. Small eclectic bars and restaurants will infuse your nightlife after you've hiked a mountain rainforest trail, dived at a world-acclaimed dive site or just lazed by a pool with a good book.*

That was okay. That didn't sound gay, and I sure as hell needed to relax and read a bit. I'd wanted a break, and both Pablo and the store were taken care of. I'd come this far. I wasn't that hot that some horny gay guy would try to rape me. I would just swear Nelson to secrecy that we'd gone to a gay resort. Aw, heck. I had two friends left in the world . . . three including Nelson. Suddenly, it pissed me off that my so-called pals had dumped me because they thought I was gay. I'd been too busy licking my wounds and putting out financial fires to lift my head from the quicksand to realize I'd been ostracized.

"What's the word around Ojai about me?" I asked Nelson. His focus was back on the movie so it took him a few seconds to listen to my repeated question. He shrugged.

"Everyone says you're a great guy."

"For a homo?"

He laughed. "No. the only one who made a comment about that was Joe. He didn't believe it. He said his gaydar didn't flare up around you."

"Why did you two break up?"

Nelson's eyes clouded for a moment. "He hooked up with his ex on Facebook."

Ouch. "Well," I said. "I'm here now. I guess I should give

Saba a chance."

"Good." He returned his attention to his movie.

I wrestled with my thoughts and some increasingly funny emails from Ellis. My teen thieves had returned to the store. I'd warned him about them. He'd shamed them into paying for the book they'd pinched. Either that or returning it. He pointed to a spot in the wall and said they'd been caught on tape. They would have been, had there actually been a hidden camera there.

He told me they paid him on the spot.

They spent a lot of time trying to see the hidden camera.

I laughed out loud and typed back, *I wish I'd thought of that idea myself. I plan to install one as soon as I return.*

Ellis fired back with, *Now they think you're cool. Word will spread. Nobody will steal from you. How does it feel being out of the closet, by the way, for all of twelve minutes?*

I wrote back, *Fuck you :)*

Ellis wrote: *My goodness. You just busted outta that closet and you're already wanting to stick your dick in me?*

I laughed and caught Nelson laughing, too, only he was laughing at the movie, not the email, or so I thought.

"Your friend has a good sense of humor," he said when I turned off the laptop.

Our arrival in Miami meant several hours of downtime. The vacation package Nelson had won included a night's stay at a motel airport. Neither of us was thrilled about the sound of planes soaring past the windows of the motel-check in desk, but I was very happy with the thought of two double beds.

"You sure you don't want to share a king?" Nelson asked me. "The king comes with complimentary champagne."

"No, thank you."

"I promise I can keep my hands off you."

"Yeah you will." I was starting to sweat. I did not want to

share a bed with him. I wanted to sleep alone. Naked. Near an ocean breeze.

We took the two-bed room, dumped our stuff, and then sat on the beds, contemplating the airport view.

"It's only for tonight," Nelson said. "You want to grab a drink?"

Six o'clock was the cocktail hour, and we found a bar nearby. Nelson seemed perfectly comfortable downing a beer and chatting about the weird things he'd seen as a vet.

"You mean the dog that ate all those coins last night wasn't the weirdest?" I asked.

"Heck, no. There's a dog who steals ladies' underwear living in our neighborhood."

"Really? Which one?"

"I don't want to out him. He gets awfully embarrassed when I have to help pull a g-string from his ass."

That made me laugh. Nelson was a cool guy.

One of the bar patrons mentioned how he'd had a black widow spider crawl out of his ear canal and that it kept him freaked out for days. He insisted on showing us the footage he captured via his camera phone and it scarred me for life.

"Well, that was creepy," Nelson said. "I bet you thought there were more in there."

"I sure did." The guy still looked wide-eyed at the memory. "I flushed my ears for days."

Nelson and I grabbed a couple more beers and relocated to one of the beer garden tables outside. Adele was singing "Someone Like You" and it dampened my mood only momentarily. Some tacos and enchiladas mellowed me out. I enjoyed talking to Nelson. He was smart and fun, and had he not told me he was gay, I'd never have guessed it.

Back in our room, we took turns taking showers. He was already asleep by the time I emerged, ready for bed. I sat propped with a couple of pillows at my back, plugged in my earphones and watched back-to-back episodes of *Orange is the New Black* on my laptop, thanks to Netflix.

I hardly ever sat through an entire episode of anything. At home I always found things to fix or clean, or otherwise do. I stretched out and almost screamed when my toe connected with something fuzzy beneath the sheets. I pushed back the covers hoping it wasn't a black widow spider.

No. It was a woman's hair band. What the hell was it doing in my supposedly clean sheets? I didn't sleep too well after that. I dropped off around five o'clock in the morning, only to be woken by Nelson.

"Wakey wakey! We're off to Saba Island!" He ran off for another shower, and I wanted to punch out his lights for being so perky.

Half an hour later, we grabbed cups of complimentary coffee in the lobby. A maid passed us by and I recognized the band in her hair as being the twin of the one I'd found in my sheets. Suddenly, my ear tickled and I slapped it.

"You okay?" Nelson asked me, biting into an apple.

"Yeah. I keep thinking about the guy with the black widow spider."

"Wasn't that gross?" He eyed the fruit bowl. "Have an apple. The pectin will calm you down."

"Really?"

"No." He shrugged. "But it sounded good, didn't it?"

I laughed. He was a character for sure.

The shuttle collected us at six, right on time for our seven a.m. flight to Philipsburg, St. Maarten. The air was soft and warm, carrying a sense of expectation for me. The final flight of our journey was exciting for about ten minutes. I started to fret that other travelers would think Nelson and I were a couple. The entire plane seemed filled with straight couples on their honeymoons. There were also a few pairs of giggling girls, the kind you often see on package tours. A fleeting memory of my honeymoon in Maui with Sam flashed through my mind. I remembered a couple of European girls falling down drunk in our spa resort bar. Sam and I had made sure they got safely got to their room. Here I was, five years later, on another exotic trip, only this time I was alone and people thought I was gay. I could see my immediate future, one of walking with my back against walls and a long-term residence tucked inside my suitcase for my box of condoms.

We arrived just in time for the connecting bus that would take us to Simpson Bay for the final portion of our journey . . . the morning fairy to Saba Island. I was astonished to learn it was a two and a half hour ride. Nelson nudged me as we joined the line in the breezy gateway and handed me a pill and a fresh bottle of water.

"What's that?" I asked, hoping it wasn't ecstasy.

"Meclizine," he said. "For sea sickness. We'll need it. Everyone says the ferry ride is horrendous."

"Oh, now you tell me." I popped the pill, and he took one, too. The ferry looked snazzy and sleek, all white with orange stripes. It was okay for about half an hour, but then several of us started to react to the abrupt choppiness of the waves and the ferry's slapping bounce on the water's surface.

I tried to focus on the beautiful view of ocean and islands in the distance. My stomach rumbled and all of a sudden I felt great. A few people stuck their heads over the sides of the ferry and barfed, but Nelson and I closed our eyes and didn't look. I've always found barfing and yawning to be contagious.

At Saba's tiny harbor, the dazzling mountains ahead of us captured everyone's attention. Nelson and I were picked up by the dreadlocked driver from our hotel. He waited on the edge of the sand with a sign that said Blue Hills Resort, but with the rainbow flag above it, the sign might have screamed, *GAY*.

"Welcome to Saba Island, Mon," he said. "I'm Jimmy, and I'll be your driver this morning." He had an engaging smile and big hands that made light work of taking custody of our bags.

Jimmy walked us to his bright pink bus—God help us it couldn't have been more pink if we'd tipped a gallon of Pepto Bismol over it. I watched him stow the suitcases with awe at the twelve suitcases belonging to the only other people on the bus, two men who had a slight aura to them. Nelson was riveted and I wondered if the guys were movie stars. We climbed on board and headed along a smooth road.

I studied the swaying palm trees outside the windows and ignored the furtive groping inside the bus. Nelson was sprawled across two seats on the other side of the bus, pretending to sleep, but he was actually fixated on the couple who sat ahead of him. One man had dark hair and was pretty muscular, while his companion was slim and blond.

They kissed, groped and bopped along to Bob Marley, and Jimmy air-drummed as he drove.

We arrived at a huge, white hotel with crimson awnings. Perched on a cliff's edge, it looked like something out of a tropical painting. Could it really be this stunning? I was slack-jawed, taking in the impressive paradise of trees and plants surrounding the place.

"Don't you know who those guys are?" Nelson asked as we got off the bus.

I shook my head. We waited for Jimmy to lug their stuff into the lobby.

"They're major gay porn stars." Nelson looked ecstatic. "The dark-haired guy is Rex Rogan and the twink is his boyfriend, Quinn Brody."

"Okay," I said. I didn't care who they were. I wanted something to eat. "Do you suppose we can get food here or will we need to leave the hotel?"

"Ooh, I was just wondering the same thing."

Jimmy rushed back out and fished in the bus's cargo hold for our bags. I wondered if he was gay or straight.

Inside the hotel, the porn power couple was still checking in.

The driver was so mesmerized by the duo he tripped over his own feet. I stared at the blond. Nelson had called him a *twink*. I guessed it meant he was kind of a cupcake. He turned and caught me staring at me, and gave me the most disarming smile. His face was lovely. There was something sad and wistful about the guy. I smiled back.

"They broke up recently," Nelson said as we walked into the hotel. "It was all over the Internet. Guess they got back together."

I was way more interested in our surroundings than *Gays of Our Lives*. I was surprised how stunning and lush the resort was. Once we stood in the gracious lobby with overhead wooden fans moving at an easy, hypnotic pace, I couldn't think of any good reason to insist on going home. Besides, I was exhausted.

The porn couple was still checking in. We overheard the desk clerk telling them the Hideaway Café was open for lunch.

"We have three cafés here, but the Hideaway is our most popular. Everything is organically prepared."

"Fabulous." The twink turned and gave us a wave.

"Enjoy your vacation," he said. His voice shocked me. He looked pretty and boyish, but he had a very deep voice.

We checked in, and the desk clerk went over all the paperwork Nelson handed him. He gave us key cards to our bungalow and told us we could use credit cards in the hotel but cash was always welcome. "The U.S. dollar is the official currency here. We faded out the use of the Netherlands Antillean guilder a few years ago."

"But Dutch is still the official language, isn't it?" Nelson asked. I'd forgotten that the islands were Dutch-owned.

"Yes, but English is unofficially the language most spoken here. Enjoy your vacation, gentlemen. Please let me know if I can help you in any way." He handed us a small map with arrows pointing the way to our bungalow.

"Thanks," we said in unison and walked out of the hotel along a flower-lined path.

"Let's dump our stuff and go get something to eat," Nelson said.

Cool. I was starving since we'd had little to eat on the plane. The for-purchase snack boxes had been denied us because the flight was too short, and the free snacks hardly made a dent in my hunger.

I was entranced by our two-bedroom bungalow. A basket of fresh fruit and bottle of champagne awaited our arrival. A nice touch. I let Nelson have first choice of the rooms, but both had endless views of the ocean, private terraces and nice, big plasma TVs. I had my own bathroom so I started feeling guilty about my worries that Nelson would try and bust in on me as I showered each day.

"Ready?" he asked.

We found our way to the Hideaway Restaurant. The porn couple had just walked in. Quinn turned and gave us another electric smile.

"You have to join us," he said, as if seeing us again was the most exciting thing that had ever happened to him. I was amazed how nice he was. His boyfriend was a little more quiet. Actually, he seemed to be kind of full of himself. I noticed he kept catching his own gaze in the mirrored walls. He was a good looking guy if you like that big slab of muscle look. I felt a lot more at ease with Quinn, who laughed a lot, though a hint of sadness still lingered in his eyes. There was something very approachable about him.

Quinn told me they lived in Miami and traveled the country shooting movies. Some they did together, some they did apart from each other.

"We've been together a whole year," Quinn told me. "That's a record for him."

"Don't you get jealous, watching him having sex with other men?" I asked.

"We don't watch each other's scenes. It causes too many arguments." Quinn let loose with that boyish laugh again. I caught his lover's grin.

"No," Rex said. "We don't. He tells me who he has a scene with and I stick my fingers in my ears." He gave us a demonstration and the four of us laughed. I realized was Rex was just shy. I found that endearing, a socially awkward porn personality.

I studied the menu and noticed the restaurant was open until two a.m. It made a nice change to hit a restaurant that didn't close at eight p.m. I loved Ojai, but the night life there was non-existent.

We ordered cocktails, Quinn urging me to try a Big Bamboo. I figured that was a drink and not his boyfriend's erect penis, so I happily agreed. Quinn was fun, easy company and I enjoyed talking to him. Nelson seemed to be getting along great with Rex. Once Quinn and I discovered we both had cats, our friendship seemed sealed.

"I have a Maine Coon called Junior," he said.

"Why's he called Junior?" Our drinks had just arrived and my Big Bamboo packed quite a rum-punch. *I'm chatting with a gay porn star about cats!*

Quinn glanced at his lover and laughed. "Should I tell him, sweetie?"

Rex grinned. "Sure."

"Junior stares at himself in the mirror all day long, just like Rex."

I laughed so hard rum came up through my nose.

When Quinn heard that I, too, had a Maine Coon he wanted to set up a date between our cats.

"Junior needs a boyfriend," he insisted.

"But Pablo isn't gay," I said. "Neither am I."

Quinn and Rex just laughed and ordered another round of drinks. I'd somehow slurped down an entire, gigantic cocktail and was feeling no pain. So I laughed right along with them. Our second round of drinks arrived with a tray of appetizers. The jumbo shrimp and juicy pieces of grilled lobster were the perfect accompaniment.

"Why do you think it's funny that I'm not gay?" I asked Quinn. I was aware of slurring my words, but by then I think we were all a bit hammered. I'd never had over-proof rum before. It needed a warning label: *Makes the drinker inclined to say really dumb stuff.*

I tried to rest my elbow on the table and put my chin on my wrist. Somehow I missed and banged my head on the table.

"Everybody says they're straight," Rex observed when I brought my head back up again.

"But I am straight," I bleated.

"Oh, they all say that. Especially in gay porn. They all claim to be gay for pay but the reality is they're g-a-y."

"Really?" My cheeks felt like they were on fire. "But I'm not gay. Honest."

He gave me a pitying look.

"Your ex-wife says you are," Nelson reminded me.

"Because she was cheating on me." Suddenly the world was a gloomy place again. I longed for a world like my comic books where people had quests and dreams, where there was a place for nobility in the world. And nobody had pimply asses.

I thought about the coyote and tears sprang to my eyes.

"Darling," Quinn said, his hand covering mine. "I hate to

break it to you, but you are *so* gay."

I didn't take offense. I was way too tipsy for that. I just laughed. The others laughed, too. Our waiter brought us a basket of johnnycakes.

"Oh, look," Nelson said to me, "they've named this delicious thing after you!" It was delicious, too. Johnnycakes were warm flat bread chunks made of cornmeal. I could have eaten two whole baskets myself. We ordered pizza. The waiter suggested the house special, which came with barbecued chicken and peas. I was surprised how wonderful it was. Afterward, Quinn and I split a dish of chocolate ice cream. He told me all about his hateful childhood in Kansas and how his life with Rex was so fantastic. Meanwhile, I caught Rex nuzzling and groping Nelson, who looked like a drunken deer in the headlights.

"Yes," Quinn went on, either oblivious, or extremely tolerant. "I wasn't really alive until I met Rex. He's my world."

I didn't know what to say to that. I felt like Dorothy who'd stumbled into Munchkinland. Wait, did thinking about the ultimate gay heroine make me . . . gay?

"What do you folks do back in the real world?" Quinn asked.

Well put. This felt like an isolated fantasy. We were in a dazzling, wonderful tropical dream, trapped in brilliant, bold hues, but none of it was real. I declined a third cocktail but the others drank on.

Nelson said, "I'm a vet and Johnny owns a comic book café."

"Fabulous," Quinn trilled. "I adore comic books. I read tons of them."

"You do?" That piqued my interest.

He nodded. "I love graphic novels."

"Yes, he does," Rex said, lifting his hand away from Nelson's crotch. "Me, I don't read anything more complicated than dinner menus."

"I write some," I said. "Graphic novels, I mean. Not menus."

"You do?" Quinn seemed intrigued. "Which ones?"

"The *Gangsta Guys*." It seemed too much to hope that he'd heard of my series.

He slapped my arm. "Shut up! I love those books. I loved the first one, where they were Vikings. And, oh, I just bought the inter-galactic one but I haven't read it yet."

"Really?" I was so geeked.

"You write graphic novels?" Nelson asked. "I had no idea."

"How could you not know that? Wait . . . you mean you're really not a couple?" Rex asked.

We shook our heads.

"Dang. So you really are straight?"

We told them our story. I had a good laugh until Rex leaned over to me and said, "You'll have yourself a gay encounter by the time you leave Wells Bay. Trust me on that. Even if I have to see to it myself."

CHAPTER THREE

"He was joking," Nelson said for the hundredth time back in our bungalow.

It didn't sound like it to me. I flung myself on the sofa, while Nelson slid into an easy chair. The room was really comfortable.

"Let's go for a walk," he said. "Check out the sights."

That sounded great to me. We slapped on hats and grabbed our shades and left the hotel. The sun beat down on us, but the breeze from the ocean was glorious. We soon learned via the map Nelson got hold of that Wells Bay was the only beach on the island. We passed dozens of tiny white-painted, red-roofed cottages peppering tiny, steep roads that all looked over the gorgeous ocean framed by the deep-jade green mountains.

"I'd love to go to the volcano," Nelson said.

"Not me. Things that go bang make me nervous."

He laughed. "You've got such a great sense of humor.

I did? I was dead serious!

We kept walking. "The last census showed thirteen hundred people live here," he said. "Have you noticed most of the vehicles are tour vans? They discourage residents and visitors from driving here." He checked the map. "Oh, look. This is supposed to be a great trail here." He suddenly darted to the left and I followed him through an unmarked opening between two trees.

"The trail is called Bottom Mountain," he called over his shoulder.

Uh-oh. Was that something gay?"

He walked fast and I followed, surprised at the difficulty of the climb.

"It's a two-hour walk and the toughest one on the island," he told me when we paused before entering the rainforest portion of the walk. By this time even he was in awe of our surroundings and slowed down some to take it all in. We walked through a well-defined mossy trail that had spread up and around trees. The branches were gigantic, and a couple of banyans had spread their roots everywhere. It was quite dark the farther we went, fog drifting in small gusts through the forest. Suddenly, we glimpsed the rooftops of a small group of gingerbread cottages far below us to our right.

"Ah, according to the map, this is the town of St. Johns," Nelson said. I felt a bit like Hansel and Gretel as jewel-toned oleander and bright, gigantic hibiscus flowers of every hue greeted us. The air seemed to hum with joy. We hiked all the way to the bottom of the mountain to the ocean. Peeling out of our clothes down to our underpants, we left our things on a pile of rocks and jumped into the water.

It was lovely. I wished we'd brought water to drink, but the swim refreshed us. We put our clothes on again and began to hike back, surprising a family that was coming from the other direction.

"You fellows need water?" the father asked, handing us a bottle of water.

"Oh, thank you," I said and snapped the cap, guzzling half. I handed it to Nelson who finished it off.

"Thanks," he said. When the family passed us, he studied the map again.

"Bottom is the name of the main town on the island he said. "Way over there is the Queen's Garden Resort. Why don't we go grab a coffee or a drink?"

"Sounds good." We kept moving, Nelson clutching the empty bottle. We arrived at the resort an hour later. But now it was almost seven and the sun was starting to dip into the sea.

The place was gorgeous, and just as inviting as our hotel. It had a timeless charm to it, as though we'd stepped back to a gentler era.

"You feel like dinner?" Nelson asked.

I sure did. "Are we dressed for it, though?"

"Of course we are," he said.

Our evening meal in that incredible restaurant was one I will never forget. The view from the windows was so breathtaking I never wanted to leave. Nelson and I ordered the evening special of snapper, which arrived with risotto and vegetables. I'd never liked risotto, but this was spectacular. Creamy and beautifully seasoned, it went down like custard. Outside, a few couples perched in the romantic Bird's Nest tables nestled up high in a deck built into a century-old mango tree. It made me want to be in love and nuzzling someone wonderful up there.

Not that I didn't enjoy Nelson's company. We spoke so easily together, never running out of things to talk about. Nelson was an ardent animal lover and fretted each time a live lobster was removed from the restaurant tank to be boiled alive.

"I know I'm eating fish but I tell myself it was killed humanely," he said.

When I told him I felt the same way he shook his head. "I knew you were a cool guy."

We each drank a glass of crisp white wine, enjoyed the palate cleanser of champagne sorbet, then chose a dessert to share. I let Nelson pick and he selected a chocolate ganache basket topped with fresh fruit. I'd never enjoyed a meal more in my life, nor was I more grateful when Nelson suggested a taxi for our return trip to Blue Hills.

Back in our bungalow, I was exhausted, but happily so. It was ten o'clock and I was happy to prepare for bed. I took a shower, washing away the day. No spiders. Thank God. I dried off, threw on a T-shirt and shorts, giving myself over to the moonlight view from my terrace. The ocean beckoned below, the cool breeze fluttering across my skin. I'd sleep with the windows open, allowing the ocean's roar to lull me to sleep.

I found the TV remote and turned on the plasma. A gay porn video was playing. Holy cow! It was Rex and Quinn. Rex was lying on his back, a glazed look of lust on his face. Quinn sat astride him, looking down into his lover's face. Oh, my God, they were being spied on! I sat up and Nelson showed up at my bedroom door, dressed in jeans and a white T-shirt.

"Are you watching gay porn?"

"No." I fumbled with the remote. "I turned on the TV and look—it's Quinn and Rex."

He glanced at the screen. "Oh, that's one of their first movies."

I stared at him. "How do you know?"

He grinned. "I've seen 'em all. Listen, they invited me over for . . ." He blushed. " . . . a little nightcap."

"A nightcap? Is that what gay people call a threesome these days?"

He laughed. "That's what we call a little after-dinner drink." He gave me a finger wave. "Ciao. Don't wait up."

"I won't." I changed channels to the tune of his retreating footsteps. From somewhere across the arc of bungalows, all facing the ocean, I heard the impassioned cries of a man.

"Fuck the hell out of me, David!"

We sure as hell aren't in Kansas anymore, Toto.

I felt restless. A long shower didn't help me feel any sleepier. I turned down the bed and slipped between the sheets. Oh yeah, these were some expensive linens. My toes enjoyed the silken feel of the thread-count. I changed channels and found an old episode of *Charmed*. I watched two of them back-to-back. At three a.m., still wide awake, I felt restless. It was hard to describe the sensation. It wasn't that I waited for Nelson so much as I waited for . . . something to happen. I switched on the bedside lamp and got out of bed. I padded over to my laptop, which was recharging on the small writing table in my room. I switched it on.

Free WiFi. Cool. No messages. Huh.

I checked the daily news from Ojai. It saddened me to see the foreclosure listings. No. I wouldn't look. I shut the computer down after sending Ellis a message letting him know we'd arrived. I got back into bed, changing channels again. What the hell was I doing watching campy TV shows in an all-gay resort?

Maybe I should look into getting a ferry back to St. Maarten and the first available flight out of Philipsburg. That thought calmed me, but sleep had started to overtake me. I drifted off, aware of Nelson returning to the bungalow some time later.

The sun awakened me. Music blared from somewhere, jolting me out of my peaceful dreams. Someone else yelled, "Shut up!" I got out of bed and looked out the window that led to my balcony. I wore my boxer briefs and figured that was decent enough if anyone saw me. The music came from Quinn and Rex's bungalow. At least I assumed it was theirs, because they were naked on their balcony, the next one over from mine, dancing to Bob Marley's "One Love."

"Is that you making that racket?" Nelson asked, storming into my room. Holy shit, he was naked, and I was surprised to see he had a massive cock.

"Of course not," I said. "It's your boyfriends next door."

He looked grumpy. "Man, I've had no sleep. What time is it?"

I checked my clock radio. "Seven o'clock."

Nelson shook his head. "I'm going back to bed."

"You get lucky last night?" I asked.

His goofy grin told me all I needed to know. "They're pretty hot," he said.

I shook off the imagery filtering uninvited into my mind.

He went off to his room and I got back into bed. I should get online and check on flights leaving St. Maarten. I kept telling myself this, but I drifted off to sleep once the music died down next door. By the time I awoke two hours later, I felt refreshed and got out of bed to take a proper look at my view. I was amazed at the beauty before me. Down by the shore, fishing boats lined the harbor and I watched women in colorful, long dresses barter with the crews holding up nets containing fish, crabs and lobster.

The ocean sparkled in the distance. The crescent-shaped bay beckoned like a shiny emerald. I looked to my left and almost fell over.

Nelson was lying on a chaise, naked. Quinn knelt on the terrace floor, between his legs, sucking his cock. Nelson made a lot of moaning noises and next thing I knew, Rex came out to the balcony, still naked, sporting a raging hard-on. He held a bottle of champagne and three glasses. Nelson reached over and grabbed the guy's cock. Man, it was like watching a bad porn movie. What was I thinking? They were porn stars!

For a moment, I stared, as if I was witnessing the scene of a car crash.

Nelson sucked Rex's length into his mouth. Rex stroked Nelson's head, then looked across and saw me watching them.

"Hey," he shouted. "Come on over!"

Never. Not on your life. I backed away, crashing into the balcony door in my haste to get back into my room. I turned on the computer. I had to get out of here. Today. To my dismay, my dream holiday had become one big gay Mardi Gras nightmare. Some week-long Saban carnival was taking place starting tomorrow. And I was dismayed to learn that the ferry only left the island every three days. *Three days!* I freaked. Not only did there appear to be very few available hotel rooms in the entire area thanks to the upcoming festivities, but the ones I found were exorbitant. Not only that but I couldn't get a flight out of St. Maarten for at least a week.

For several long minutes, I contemplated my options.

An email popped up from Ellis.

Stop stressing. Have fun and relax.

I went nuts and typed back something rude and derogatory. Then my cell phone rang.

"Dude," he said, "Will you get over yourself? Women have screwed you over. Just enjoy. I'd give anything to change places with you."

"Why? What's the matter?" I panicked that something was wrong.

"Nothing's the matter. I just, well . . . I don't want to go home yet, and if Gen thinks you're coming home then I'll have to go back to Club Lesbo."

"Club Lesbo?"

"Yeah, her friend that's visiting just happens to be the chick my wife had a brief Sapphic fling with in college, only the friend thinks that she can maybe lure Gen back into the sheets."

"Are you sure you should have left them alone together?" I was alarmed now.

"Hey, you were right there with Sam and she still bonked Frankie."

That was true enough.

"Hi," he said, finally, "I think you should just get drunk

and look for some cool chicks."

"Yeah. You're right." I warmed to the idea. "I can do that."

He still sounded down.

"Gen found her friend on Facebook. Fuck I hate the Internet. The social fucking cheaters network."

I did, too. That was how Frankie, my old college buddy, came back into my life and stole it from me.

"There's some big-time festival here," I said. "Maybe I'll get lucky."

"You do that," Ellis said. "Pablo and I are gonna watch some TV. I ordered a pizza."

"Pizza?" I checked my watch. It was almost midnight there.

"Yeah, and spaghetti and meatballs and a sub."

"Holy cow. Are you going to eat all that?"

"Abso-fucking-lutely. Gen keeps me on a low sodium diet so I'm going nuts here. Pablo likes the pepperoni. Is it okay if I let him have some?"

"Sure," I said. Heck, even my cat was a slut. I began to worry about what would happen when I got home and stopped giving Pablo people food.

I turned on the radio in my room just in time to hear an announcer say, "Up from The Bottom to Zion's Hill; down from Hell's Gate to the slopes of St. Johns; from the quaint shops and homes of Windwardside to the deep blue shores of Cove Bay; from the top of the kingdom's highest peak of Mt. Scenery to the industrial buzz at Fort Bay Harbor, the call is going out for the diverse parts of the island community to come together to Fete and Spree in Unity to celebrate the fortieth Annual Saba Summer Carnival Festival."

Wow, it sounded spectacular.

A knock on my door got my attention. I turned and found Nelson, a towel wrapped around his waist, looking cool as the proverbial cucumber.

"It's the Saba Island Annual Carnival," he said. "Wanna come with us? It's supposed to be really fun."

"Sure," I said. "I thought it was starting tomorrow, but according to the radio it's on."

"Yeah. This year they extended it from eight days to eleven. It's started already."

I figured I was safe with anything that kept us away from bedrooms or private terraces. He gave me a bright smile, then went off to change.

I shucked off my pajama bottoms and dressed in Bermuda shorts and a Hawaiian shirt. I found him in the living room snacking on a banana.

"Ready?" he asked.

"As I'll ever be."

He finished the banana and chewed the inside of the skin before dumping it in the waste basket. "All the enzymes are in the skin," he said.

"I didn't know that." I had no idea really what he normally ate, but he was a specimen. How cow. Was that a gay thought? No, I told myself. A man could appreciate another man's physical appearance without being gay.

In the lobby, I spotted our driver from the previous day. Jimmy gave us a friendly wave and I noticed him carrying in a large collection of designer luggage. Did he work around the clock?

Outside the hotel, Rex sat in the driver's seat of a Jeep, Quinn beside him. Jimmy roared off in his pink bus, waving to us all. We waved back. Nelson and I climbed into the back seat of the Jeep. We took off, a blast of reggae music accompanying us on the radio. Rex seemed to know his way around the island and tore along the road. A woman in a long, colorful dress, balancing a basket on her head filled with fruit and vegetables, walked beside the road. She gave us a smile, even though we barely missed hitting her by inches. Wow, the Sabans really were a laid-back people. Back home, even in Ojai, that would get you the finger at the very least.

We motored through a narrow road with thick foliage. Quinn turned out to be a noisy, but accurate, backseat driver. Rex was like my dad, the ultimate macho guy who refused directions, got lost and had to backtrack. Not that I minded. I was dazzled by the profusion of colors. Birds, flowers, trees, the sky . . . everything was bluer here. The music rolled on, everything sounding the same, but somehow appropriate to the stunning views.

"That's it," Rex said, "I told you I'd find it." We shot forth between a thatch of bamboo and wound up in the middle of a pineapple patch.

"Oops," he said.

The rest of us laughed. He backed out again and we found our way to the festival. Music, dancing, drumming, eats. I headed straight for the food stalls, finding myself bopping along to the music. I noticed people lining up for ackee, which I quickly learned was the staple island fruit. Here it came in hot, flaky buns with a custard sauce. I mowed through three of them, then noticed Quinn staring at me.

"Everything okay?" I asked him.

"I'd love to have one of those," he said. He looked so forlorn I couldn't believe it.

"They come in a bag of six. Here, have one."

The ackee had an unusual taste. Almost like scrambled eggs.

"I can't eat stuff like that. My staple diet is crushed ice and cigarettes." He looked so longingly at the bag that it wasn't hard to convince him to take a bite of one.

"Also sperm," he said.

"Sperm?" I tried not to laugh. "How many calories in that?"

"The average man is around seventy calories a load."

"What's your daily caloric intake?" I asked.

"Of sperm? Mm, I'm not sure. Depends, but around a thousand calories."

I couldn't respond. For some reason the whole discussion had me laughing.

"The ackee's not bad," he said. "Kind of eggy. Kind of . . . spermy."

That set us both off into fits of laughter.

We had a long discussion about the taste of fruit. I had nothing to contribute to his observations on sperm. He took a second bite of the bun in his hand and almost screamed when Rex caught up with us. He had no qualms finishing the bun, and then filched another one. I didn't care. I hurried over to buy fried plantains. I was in food heaven. The festival began and I watched the dancers, enchanted by the small children in colorful garb.

People had fun and, oh my God, I could smell marijuana. I accepted a fruity drink from Nelson and realized after a long sip that it contained rum. Between that and the heavy ganja fumes I became the life of the party. I joined the conga line and chugged down my rum drink with one hand, gripping the hip of a rather large woman in front of me with the other.

Nelson held onto me from behind, his throaty laughter igniting my own. I somehow knew the lyrics to the song booming over the crowd, and my hips and feet beat out in time to the music.

Rex caught up with us, handing us fresh drinks. I was beginning to like the guy. We all wound up dancing and swaying by a sea cove.

I sat on the rocks, watching Rex and Quinn skinny dipping. Nelson stripped off, too. I was a little shyer about being naked around them all. I no longer feared gay rape, I just hadn't been naked around an adult man. Ever.

"Come on," Nelson coaxed. "Come for a swim."

I put down my empty drink cup and abandoned my shorts and shirt. I joined the others in the sea, an amazing sense of freedom hitting me as the waves pounded us. We laughed and splashed and kept shouting out silly things to one another. We climbed out again, sitting on the rocks. I lay back, my head under my arms and enjoyed the sun.

The sounds of sex jolted my eyes open. I sat up, dismayed to see the other three getting it on. What was with them and their non-stop sex party? Nelson lay on the rocks, Rex kneeling beside him, holding Nelson's cock in his hand. Quinn lay close to Nelson, kissing his mouth. He moved down, taking Nelson's left nipple into his mouth. I watched. The sensuousness of the scene didn't escape me.

"Taste him," Rex said, nudging his lover.

Quinn moved down and took custody of Nelson's cock with his eager mouth. Nelson cried out, his head lifting from the rock for a moment. I watched, mesmerized as his hand moved down Quinn's back, his thumb stroking the man's spine. It was a slow, seductive sweep of his fingers, his hand resting at Quinn's shapely ass crack.

"Touch him for me," Rex ordered Nelson, whose fingers delved a little deeper.

Rex pushed his lover away and took over the cock-sucking duties. I didn't want to watch three men having sex, but I also couldn't stop watching. I noticed to my horror that I had a hard-on.

The scene in front of me turned frenzied within seconds. I pushed my cock down, covering it up with my folded arms. Rex moved off Nelson's cock, and up to his face. He offered Nelson his cock. Nelson moaned as he sucked it in, his own cock disappearing into Quinn's mouth again.

I couldn't watch. I was shocked by my body's reaction and my emotional one. I realized to my dismay I was jealous.

Knowing the other three were in their own little world allowed me to leave without them noticing. Nelson's throaty sounds seem to soar across the island. All I could hear was ecstatic man-moans and furious cock sucking. I pulled my clothes back on and beat a hasty retreat. I tried to analyze the root of my feelings. I felt a bit abandoned and ignored. That's all it was. We were having fun and they all had to go turn it into their own personal porn scene. I had to admit it was erotic, if you liked that sort of thing.

My cock was still hard, wedged uncomfortably in my shorts. I got hard and horny, I decided, because I hadn't had sex in six months. As I clambered over the rocks, I realized it had been longer than that. For the last couple of months we'd been together, Sam had acted like sex was akin to hard labor. Of course I didn't know then that she was having an affair and didn't want to cheat on her lover, with me, her husband. That revelation when it finally tumbled out had been devastating. I hadn't even jacked off since then. It was unnatural for a man. I needed to go back to the room, take a shower and talk to the hand.

At the top of the ridge, I jumped back as an island Jeep nearly ran me over.

"Sorry, Mon!"

"Watch it!" I shouted. I was sobering up fast.

The Jeep crunched to a halt.

"Johnny, Mon?"

I stepped forward. "Jimmy?"

He turned and waved, his white teeth gleaming.

"Wasn't sure it was you," he shouted over his raucous reggae. "You bald-heads all look alike to me."

"Bald-heads? I'm not bald."

"That's what we call whites." The grin was disarming. "Get in, Mon."

I did. We took off so fast I almost fell out the door.

"Breathe easy, Mon." His voice was smooth and mellow.

"Where are we going?" I asked over the music.

"Cove Bay."

"What is that? I heard it mentioned on the radio."

"A nice place to hang out. I have a little picnic in back." He jabbed his thumb over his shoulder.

"You seem to work a lot, I'm glad you have time for a picnic."

He turned the music down. "Seriously, yeah, Mon. I worked right up until half an hour ago. Filling in for guys that went missing. Too much ganja."

I nodded. I could imagine it would be hard to stick to a schedule here in paradise. So far I hadn't written a single word since I'd arrived.

"Balance," he said.

I looked at him. What the hell was he talking about?

"Balance?"

"Yeah. Be chillin'. In all things. You look for balance."

"I see." I thought about it. Okay, so he was a bit of a philosopher.

"Balance. I like that."

Cove Bay was all of five minutes' drive from the place I'd swum with the others, but it was simply spectacular. The waves crashed against a tiny, pristine slice of sand that contained no footprints at all. It felt like our own, tiny hideaway.

We climbed down the rocks and picked a spot on the flattest one we could find to sit on. Jimmy tossed a bright yellow and blue beach blanket onto it, then he spread out a feast. I sat on the sand beside it. I didn't think I could eat again after stuffing my face earlier, but the cold chicken and crab legs were delicious. He handed me a thermos lid filled with liquid.

"Slippery nipple," he said, "my favorite cocktail."

It was delicious. It was rummy and fruity but had a smooth edge to it.

"Bailey's Irish Cream," he said, topping me up. Man, I'd be constantly intoxicated at this rate.

He poured himself a shot and stunned me by taking off all his clothes. His massive dick was the biggest I'd ever seen. It almost touched his kneecap.

"Let's swim," he said.

Fine by me. The water was warm and translucent. We splashed around and then I heard the waterfall. He inclined his head.

"Follow me."

We swam toward the sound, to a freshwater lagoon with the most beautiful, blinding foliage I'd ever seen. If I'd been with a woman I'd have wanted to make love in the soft, fragrant, blue, blue water. Instead, I was with Jimmy, and we swam around, enjoying the visual feast. We swam back to the beach and waded to shore.

Back on the sand, he reached into his basket and produced some lotion.

"We should put this on. We don't want to burn."

"You're so dark," I said. "Can you get sunburned?"

"Yes, except when I get burned, my skin kinda turns white. Not so sexy, Mon."

I laughed. He was a character. We gazed out to sea.

"How long have you lived here?" I asked as he snapped open his bottle.

"Couple of years. I'm from the islands of Turks and Caicos originally. Beautiful. But not much work. And hard for a battyman."

A what? I was about to ask, but he poured me another slippery nipple. It went straight to my head, making me smile.

"Are you batty?" he asked.

"Batty?"

He raised his eyes skyward. "Gay."

I shook my head, and his eyes seemed to cloud over.

"I'm a battyman. Di man dem beg fa jooks."

"What does that mean?"

"Are you gonna make me beg for sex?"

He leaned over me, picking up the lotion bottle.

I laughed. Obviously he was joking. He slathered some on his arms and moved over to mine. I felt his fingers working on my shoulders. It felt good having lotion rubbed into my skin as I sat in the sun. His hands moved down my back. I flashed on the moment I'd watched Nelson running his hand down Quinn's back. A tingle of fire stirred in my cock. Jimmy's hands were busy.

"You know the feet need lotion, too."

He reached down to my foot. Nobody had ever rubbed anything into my feet before. My cock jumped to attention. I was embarrassed, but Jimmy was kind enough to pretend not to notice. My cock yearned for release and, within seconds, I covered it with my arms.

"Balance," he said, brushing my arms away. "You have a nice, hard cock there, Johnny. It crawb up."

"What?"

"It looks good."

He wore an intense expression on his face as his big fingers stroked up my legs. My body began to relax. I closed my eyes and saw rainbows behind the lids as I felt his rhythmic touch on my skin. He was in no hurry, in spite of his apparent desire to get lucky. I knew I should have stopped him before he got to my thighs, but my body had a mind of its own. His fingers reached the top of my thigh and I felt the ridge of his thumb brush my ball sac.

Jimmy moved his hand down again. I sighed. My body felt pleasantly pliant and sleepy. Another upward movement and his fingers were back at my balls.

"Balance," he said and his tongue tip went straight to my cock head. His tongue felt so good against my now-baking shaft. I lay on the rock, unable . . . *unwilling* to move. I'd never had such a blowjob in my life. Fuck me. It was incredible. The man sucked me in. No teeth. He crooned over my length as he held me in his warm mouth. I felt my cock head hit the back of his throat and, oh, man, I wanted to come right then and there. His hand swept against my ball sac. I couldn't hang on any longer. My fingers flailed against the few hot grains of yellow sand I could reach. I shouted to him.

"Jimmy, I'm coming." His mouth tightened and I came deep in his throat. I couldn't believe how blissful it was. I lay back, my mouth hanging open as he released me, then began licking my cock again. Whenever I reacted to his touch, he'd lick me again in the same spot, seeming to delight in awakening my senses. My cock sprang back to life and he worked his way down, licking my balls.

My wife, in our whole entire relationship had never sucked me with such reverence or attention to my body's responses. His lips worked on the skin of my balls, pulling, teasing, taunting me to erotic heights I'd never imagined. By the time I came again, my soaking wet balls in his hand, my cock submerged in his mouth, I didn't think a second intense orgasm was possible.

Oh, but it was. He ran his free hand across my groin. I'd never felt such ripples of pleasure. I exploded in the man's mouth. When he released me, he grinned.

"I think you're a battyman."

For a long moment, I lay there, dizzy from the sensations

he'd infused in me. He lay back, a hand across his eyes.

"I don't know if I can reciprocate," I said. "You're the first man I was ever with."

"Huh," he said. "We'll see about that."

He stood, picked up our clothes, picked up our picnic things, then held out his hand to me. He picked me up, hoisting me over his shoulder. I remembered this was the guy who carried five hundred suitcases with apparent ease. He took me to the Jeep and put me into the front seat like I was fragile cargo. I reached for my clothes.

"Level," he said. I guess he noticed my confusion because he quickly translated. "Calm down."

He hopped beside me and we drove, naked, through the late afternoon sun.

"Where are we going?" I asked. He flashed me a smile. His cock was hard, his hand reaching over to mine and, oh, boy, soon, I was, too.

We reached a white cottage tucked into a curve on a hill. He parked, one hand gripping my cock. He honked his horn.

"Daddy," he shouted. "I brought you a gift!"

I sat up straight, fear mingling with the rum and sex. A big, black man came out of the cottage. I was shocked to see him walk over to Jimmy and kiss him. They came over to me and led me inside, Jimmy's hand back on my cock, our clothes under his arm.

The house was small but comfortable looking. Jimmy led me to what looked like a hammock dangling from the ceiling. He put me in it. Shit. My legs spread, my ass seemed to be hanging over the edge. I was a sitting, sprawling, sex duck. Jimmy put a kiss on my cock. It reacted in a way I could not control.

"Want a drink, Johnny?"

His hand stroked across my groin. Man, he seemed to know all my erogenous zones. Why couldn't I meet a chick who wanted to turn me on this way?

I wanted a drink, but now, the other guy's hot breath puffed onto my ass cheeks as he brushed away sand from my butt. He was so close it felt oddly alluring, and then his tongue was soon all over my ass. I almost screamed. Sam had never wanted to go near there when we were together. As the man licked me, my gaze took in the sight of a big, black man going to town with his tongue on me. It was too much to take.

"Breathe easy, just enjoy it," Jimmy said. "Oh, look, you gonna come again."

I couldn't speak. I couldn't move. I was so overcome by the sensation of a big, wet tongue in my ass, nothing else mattered. Suddenly I didn't care who was licking me, or who was making me feel this way. I wanted to come and I did *not* want the licking to stop. In my life I'd never had two people working on me. This was a fantasy, but in my mind, it usually involved a couple of chicks. Unbelievably, I came a third time, and Jimmy lifted his head, grinning at me. He wiped his mouth.

"Now you can have a drink."

He brought me a rum-punch that was about as strong as anything else I'd been drinking since I'd arrived in Saba. It was tasty, but then I felt Jimmy's partner at my ass again. I couldn't believe how horny these guys were. Jimmy had a huge erection. He smiled at me. I felt his partner trying to get his fingers into my butt and I freaked out. The hazy, lazy cloud I'd been floating on thanks to my sexual euphoria evaporated. I leaned up, my drink splashing everywhere.

I pushed the guy's hands away. I had no idea what I was doing here. I wanted to get out. Now.

"Relax, Mon. Be chillin'," Jimmy said. I was getting sick of him telling me to relax. I sat up, forcing my legs out of the awkward sling.

"He ain't fish," Jimmy's boyfriend said. He shook his head and walked away.

"Fish?" I asked, my voice coming out in a croak.

"Island speak for gay."

Christ. I couldn't cope.

"No. I'm not fish and I want to go back to the hotel." I shook with fear.

"Why are you frightened?" Jimmy looked concerned. "Chill, Mon. It be okay."

I put on my clothes. My cell phone rang as I slipped my shorts over my legs. It was Nelson.

"Where are you?" he asked. "I'm starting to get worried."

He wasn't the only one.

CHAPTER FOUR

Jimmy drove me back to the hotel a lot slower than he'd driven me to his house in the heat of sexual desire. He kept throwing looks in my direction. I felt the weight of unspoken words. I think he was afraid of saying the wrong thing to me. We turned a corner and I saw the hotel up ahead. He pulled to the shoulder of the road and turned off the ignition.

"I like you," he said. "This was supposed to be fun."

"Balance," I said.

He smiled. "That, too."

His hands gripped the steering wheel and I realized he was more upset than I thought.

"I want to see you again," he said.

"But I'm not batty."

He shrugged. "So, we have a couple of drinks and chill."

"Okay," I said, though the idea of it was not in my plans. Not at all. I just wanted things to end on a positive note. He dropped me at the hotel, cranked up his music again and tore off at his usual thrill-speed pace.

Back in the bungalow, I had no intention of telling Nelson what happened, but he must have sensed something had taken place because as soon as I walked in, he came over to me, putting his hands on my shoulders.

"You look like you've seen a ghost."

I took a deep breath. "I had sex with Jimmy."

He blinked, his eyes widening. "Big, black Jimmy? Wow, man, what was that like?"

I shook my head. I couldn't believe it had all gone down . . . or that I was repeating the whole thing to Nelson. We sat in the living room on the sofa. He faced me, his attention fully on me. It was weird. It wasn't like talking to Sam or Ellis. Sam always interrupted to ask questions. Ellis always wanted to get to the bottom line. Nelson listened and offered no comments until I'd unspooled every detail I thought I had to share. I was grateful for his silence. I was relieved not to feel any judgment.

"Man, you are something else," he said at last. "I'm pissed that Jimmy knew you were a virgin and raced you home to his old man, thinking you needed to be double-teamed that way. That must have been terrifying."

"It was," I said. "It felt good at first. Sex with a man is so different."

He smiled. "Isn't it, though?"

I relaxed completely then. I was intrigued to hear that Nelson knew about straight sex.

"Sure," he said, when I asked. "I dated women for years until I went to a gay pride festival in LA. It was Mardi Gras. A bunch of us went to dinner and there we were. I locked eyes with a guy on Santa Monica Boulevard. Only I thought he was a woman. Turned out he was a drag queen. Confused the hell out of me. I took to driving to LA every weekend to be with him. I got to explore my sexuality slowly, in private, with a wonderful man."

His voice choked. He glanced at me. "You got chucked in the deep end by a couple of crazy island guys, and you're handling yourself so well. I'm sorry they got so aggressive. Your first time shouldn't be like that."

"Thanks. It was still . . . you know . . . pretty mind-blowing, but then I haven't had sex for months. Maybe I was just damned horny."

"Maybe." He didn't look convinced. His voice turned

gentle when he asked, "How are you feeling?"

"I'm okay. I think I'm confused."

"Of course you are."

"What happened to your guy? The one in the dress?"

"Turned out he didn't like to wear dresses only for Mardi Gras. He was a full-blown cross-dresser. I respect everyone's right to their fetish but I don't want a man dressed like a woman. I like men who like to be men."

"I can understand that."

He gazed at a point in the middle distance for a moment.

"I haven't thought about Vince for a while. Talking about him still makes me sad. I had high hopes for us."

"Nelson, I'm sorry."

He shrugged. "I tried. I really did."

We sat with our thoughts a moment.

"Quinn and Rex invited us to their room for a party. You up to going?"

"No, not really. But you go ahead."

He shook his head. "Nope. Not going. I'd rather have dinner with you, if you're up for it. There's supposed to be an amazing restaurant down the road apiece. What do you say?"

"I say I love it."

He waited for me to shower and change and we left the hotel. Outside, the familiar pink bus rolled up and Jimmy's boyfriend had the wheel. He gave me a friendly wave.

"Is that the guy?" Nelson's cheek muscles twitched. "I've got half a mind to go over there and rip him a new one."

"Let's just go," I said, raising my hand in greeting. I wanted to put some distance between me and Jimmy's pal.

We walked along the road, the smell of ginger and, oddly, bread, strong on the air.

When I mentioned the bread, Nelson smiled.

"Oh, that's the breadfruit. It's been a hot day, so it's

brought out the scent of it. Breadfruit tastes like bread, too."

"I had no idea." Nelson was constantly teaching me stuff.

We reached the restaurant Brigadoon, about half a mile away. Located in a refurbished 1800's house, the terrace overlooked trees and, beyond those, the ocean. We were impressed by the menu and its mix of Creole and Caribbean food. I let Nelson order and approved of his selections of seafood jambalaya and jerk chicken and the appetizers he chose.

In spite of the lengthy wine and cocktail list, I settled for iced water since my track record for behavior once I got a bit of rum inside me had so far met with questionable results. Our waiter suggested the appetizer of coconut and garlic soup. We almost licked our bowls clean.

I glanced around us. Several couples ate by flickering candlelight. I wondered if people thought we were a couple and, for the first time, the idea didn't send me into paroxysms of anxiety. I felt soothed by the chirp of tree frogs and cicadas, the crimson sunset slipping into dark decadence.

We shared some brie with tamarind sauce, and ackee soufflé. It was superb. By the time our desserts came, the orange custard with wild-orange liqueur seemed to be the perfect ending to our meal. Nelson, however had other ideas. He ordered a snifter of Appleton 21. It was rum but its incredible smoothness tasted like cognac. We shared the same glass.

Nelson was wonderful company and I was grateful to be alone with him without Rex groping and fondling him.

"Do you find it hard being gay in Ojai?" I asked him.

"No. I find it hard being single in Ojai. Don't you?"

"To be honest, I haven't thought about it much . . . not until we talked about this trip. I've been so busy getting over my divorce and the crap Sam left behind that I haven't looked. But since you mention it, the singles scene is non-existent."

"Right. Remember Doc Garrett's foray into the bar scene?"

"Oh," I said, laughing as I thought about Doc's chichi wine bar. He thought singles from all over Ojai, Ventura and the northern beaches would flock to it. All he attracted were a few hard-core barflies who only wanted house wines and a few couples who later complained about the prices. He'd shut down six months later and I took over the premises, converting his booze bar into my comics and coffee café.

"What do you miss about Sam apart from sex?" Nelson asked.

"Not much, dude. I don't sit around thinking, 'Oh, I no longer do this or that because she's gone.'" I thought for a moment. "I miss her food. She was a damned good cook. My staple foods are grilled-cheese sandwiches and tomato soup."

He grinned. "Soup out of a can?"

I laughed. "But of course." I sipped my water. "Do you cook?"

He nodded. "I love to cook. I take cooking classes. Thai is my new thing."

"I love Thai food," I said. "Are the classes fun?"

"Oh, yes. They're the social highlight of my week. I love them. Up in Santa Barbara at the college, we have wine-tasting and pairing menus to learn."

"You'll have to cook for me some time."

The words slipped out before I could stop them.

He grinned. "Anytime. Now those classes are a social scene I can get behind."

"Ever thought about moving up there?"

He twirled his wine glass stem in his fingers.

"I have my practice. I suppose I could move . . . make the drive into Ojai every day, but I dunno . . ."

I waited him out. He sighed. "The truth is, I love Ojai. I just love the place. That's why I was excited when I met Joe. I thought he loved it, too. I love being close to Santa Barbara and Santa Ynez and all that good wine country. Being close to LA on the other side is good too. We're sort of halfway. But I always love coming home."

"Me, too," I said. "I had no idea Sam was going crazy living there."

"Yeah, Joe, too."

"Why couldn't you have been a woman?" I asked him.

"Why couldn't you have been gay?" he shot back.

I grinned. "According to my ex-wife, I am. Remember?"

He nodded. "So come on, tell me. Was the sex good today?"

"Fuck, yeah. My body's still reeling."

"Wait until you have sex with a man who loves you. You won't know what to do with yourself."

Wow. I couldn't imagine what that would be like.

"Didn't Sam do all your cooking at the café?" he suddenly asked.

"Yep."

"And now?"

"I buy ready-made sandwiches at The Cosmic Cow."

He stared at me. "You're joking."

"No, I'm not. Why?"

"Their sandwiches suck. Do you hate your customers?"

I grinned. "Only the ones that steal from me."

He looked aghast. "Does that happen a lot?"

"Enough." I gazed at him. "What about you? You have people owing you money? You get ripped off?"

"It's not so bad now that I no longer accept checks, but occasionally I get people trying to block their credit cards after they've paid me, especially when an animal dies."

"Wow. I'm sorry to hear it."

"Thanks."

"You miss Joe?" I asked him.

"I miss aspects of him, but he was a treacherous ass. It's no wonder he and Sam are friends."

"Are they still close?"

"Sure they are. He moved to LA to help her and Frankie run their new comic book store."

I stared at him.

"You seem surprised." He cocked his head to one side. "You mean you didn't know?"

I shook my head. I knew they were in LA, but I'd also heard rumors of them traveling. Sam had a Facebook page but she'd blocked me from it. She was also a voracious tweeter but she had locked her page and one needed to request her permission to follow her posts.

"You're not in contact with them at all?" he asked.

"No."

"Then why does Joe tell me she claims you're stalking her?"

He could tell by my shocked expression that the allegation was not only untrue but deeply hurtful.

"She says I'm gay but I'm also stalking her?" I couldn't hide my anger. "How does that work? She makes me sound schizo."

"I'm sorry, sweetie. I shouldn't have said anything. I didn't think it was true, but you never know."

"So," I said, trying to get off such personally painful topics. "You still talk to Joe."

"No. Not really. He emailed a couple of times and he called. I'm not sure why exactly. He's such a user. I'm not anything he's looking for. He wants rich, he wants a daddy. I'm neither of those things."

"He stays in touch because you're a great guy."

"Damn. Are you sure you're straight? 'Cos I think you're

a great guy, too."

"Yes, I'm straight."

"Well, if you ever change your stripes . . . or you want to know just how good it could be with a guy . . . I hope you'll consider me."

"If I ever do, it'll be you," I said, snatching the check before he could.

Our walk back to the hotel was easy and pleasant. I felt very comfortable with him. Back in the bungalow, I was in a mood to write. I felt a whole bunch better about my sexual tryst and, in fact, thought I'd sleep like a baby. But Cove Bay had given me some ideas for my new *Gangsta Guys* novel. I hit the computer. Nelson hovered at my bedroom door.

"Quinn called. They really want us to go over there."

"Do you mind if I stay here and write?"

"Not at all. You mind if I go?"

"Have fun," I said.

"You okay? You wanna talk some more?"

"No."

"If you do, I'm just a phone call away. My cell phone's on me. Okay?"

"Okay. And, Nelson? Thanks."

He gave me a brilliant smile. I felt weird listening to him leave. The place seemed suddenly empty. The lull of the ocean helped, and I opened up my newly-installed document file. Nelson's smile swam in my mind. I wished I could meet a woman like him. He was everything I was looking for in a partner. Hell, if I'd said to my wife that I wanted to stay home and write, she would have gone to pieces. That had been part of my problem with her. She hated my writing life. She felt it took time away from her.

I could hear the party sounds coming from next door. I tried to blot them out, but it was hard. I got some work done but I was filled with the strangest feeling of anxiety. I couldn't believe it. I took a deep breath. Then another.

Wild laughter erupted from the next bungalow. I pushed back the chair and left the room. I didn't know why I suddenly cared what he was doing, but it bothered the hell out of me that Nelson might be with another guy. Jesus, was I screwed up or what?

I rapped on the door and, to my surprise, Jimmy opened it.

Beyond him, I could see Nelson getting cozy with Rex. They stood against the wall chatting, drinks in hand. Nelson's gaze met mine and there was no mistaking the surprise and delight there.

"Listen, Mon, I'm not supposed to be here . . . you know, chillin' with the guests, okay?" Jimmy asked.

"Sure. No problem."

I moved past him. I walked right up to Nelson.

"Hey, great to see you," Rex said. "Plenty of drinks. Help yourself."

Nelson opened his mouth to say something but Rex took him away. I watched them disappear into one of the bedrooms. I stared out at the ocean. What the fuck was going on? Was I jealous?

Hell yeah, I was jealous.

Oh, fucking Christ. I think I'm a battyman.

CHAPTER FIVE

He didn't come back to the bungalow. I sort of waited up for hours, my new favorite show, *Charmed*, entertaining me at a low volume. At four a.m. I heard him coming in the front door. I leapt from the bed. My heart sank when I saw him walking in with Quinn.

"You okay?" Nelson asked, his eyes full of concern.

"Sure."

He gave me an odd look. Quinn seemed very drunk.

"Have fun," I said and went back to my room. I closed the door, lay down on my bed. And cried.

I shed a bunch of tears for my lost life, my new confusion. And Nelson. Oh, my God. Nelson. I felt I'd lost my best friend. It was the craziest feeling in the world. I wanted to say a million things to Nelson but what could I say? It was clear he didn't want me. He was with Quinn. But wait . . . hadn't he said he wished I was gay? Could I do it? Could I approach the guy and see where things went?

Ah hell. I was one mixed up country boy.

What the hell would I do if it was a disaster? I'd be running into him for the rest of my life in Ojai. Wait . . . not necessarily. I'd hardly seen him at all until he came to help the coyote. It wouldn't be so bad. But wait . . . I liked this man. I wanted his friendship. Why the fuck was I crying? Because I liked him and he was now in bed with a gay porn star!

I heard voices coming from his room. I wanted to scream. Wait. They were talking. Not moaning. I calmed down. I forced myself to breathe. I went into the bathroom and switched on the light. I looked like shit. I didn't think the stream of snot coming out of each nostril would convince Nelson to take a chance on me. I washed my face and cleaned my teeth. My eyes were still red from crying. Man, I was a wreck. I squeezed drops into my eyes, straightened my clothes and walked to his bedroom. The door was wide open.

Gone.

Man, if that wasn't the story of my life. I went back to my own room and closed the door. I swallowed down my anguish. I'd shoved all my worries, all my passion into my work. It was what I did best. Who was it that said writing was a socially acceptable form of schizophrenia?

I was amazed how much work I got done, and I sent the document file to Ellis. I checked the time. Four thirty a.m. I heard Nelson at the front door. I pushed back my chair. I found him in the hallway, swaying. He was naked from the waist up, his shirt in his hand.

Staring at him, I couldn't speak for a moment.

"What the hell did you do to yourself?" I asked.

His gaze shifted from left to right. "I shaved my head."

"Yeah, I can see that. And what the hell is that on the back of your neck?"

I turned him around. A new tattoo ran from his neck bone down between his shoulder blades. It was covered in a clear strip of plastic. The skin around it looked angry and red.

"Is that Chinese writing?"

He turned back around, nodding.

"Are you drunk?"

He gave me a loopy grin. "I sure hope so. I'd hate to think I did anything this stupid dead sober."

"What does it say?" I couldn't fathom what could have possessed him to mar his perfect physique.

"Life is hope."

"Why would you want that on your neck? You have a beautiful body. Why the hell did you do this? Did something happen? Did Quinn hurt you?"

He stared at me, his face flushed.

"Quinn?" He looked bewildered. "I don't care about Quinn."

"What about Rex?"

He burped. "'Scuse me. I've had a lot of run. I mean, rum."

"Do you like Rex?" I asked.

"He's a porn star," he said, as if that explained everything. He looked ill and rushed to his bathroom. I followed, worried about him.

"No," he said, closing the door on me.

I heard him throwing up, heard the running water and a bit more up-chucking. I paced his room. He took a shower and came back out, looking surprised to see me there.

"Johnny, does the tattoo look bad?"

"No."

"You sure?"

"Yes."

"Are you okay?" he asked.

"Uh-huh."

He pulled down the bed clothes, turned his back on me and dropped his towel. Then he pulled up black boxer briefs that were so tight I could see all the things he was packing into the tight space.

"Want to get into bed with me?" he asked.

"Yes," I said again. I tossed off everything except my own boxers and got in with him. He was the one who'd been sick, but he remained in full control. He held his arm out to me. It seemed like the most natural thing in the world to snuggle close to him, his arm holding me tight. I don't think either of us moved a muscle all night.

He was the first one up in the morning. I caught his morning wood tenting his underpants as he closed himself up in his bathroom. I considered running off to my own room but I was comfortable and, besides, the warm spot he'd left felt nice. God . . . what the hell was happening to me? I felt, rather than heard, him return to the bed. I yawned and stretched.

"How are you feeling?" I asked him.

He gave me a lazy grin. "I'm fine."

"Are you getting back in here?"

He licked his lips. "You want me to?"

Very much. "I think so, yeah."

He climbed in and I moved closer to him. He stiffened against me and not in a good way.

"What's the matter?" I asked.

"Are you kidding? We're in bed together."

"I noticed."

"Johnny. What are you doing here?"

"You invited me. Remember?"

"Yeah, but why did you say yes?"

I lifted my head and stared into his troubled eyes.

"Can't we go back to you holding me and us just being . . . close."

"This isn't a good idea."

"Why not? Don't you want me to be gay?"

He sprang out of bed. "Why are you messing with my mind?"

"I'm not messing with your mind. You're messing with mine."

"What? When? How?"

"I came to their bungalow last night and you went off with Rex. I . . . I missed you. I was . . . I was . . ." Now I felt thoroughly stupid.

"You were what?" His hands on his hips, he looked like a pissed Adonis. I wanted him. God help me. I did.

"I was jealous."

He stared at me, his hands falling to his sides.

"So I went and got drunk . . . for no reason?"

I stared up at him. The sexual and emotional tensions were so thick between us, I thought I wouldn't be able to breathe in a few minutes.

"You got drunk because of me?"

"I . . . yeah."

He sat on the bed beside me.

"Is it too late?" I asked, anxious again.

"Too late for what, Johnny?"

"For us?"

He blew out a long sigh. "If it all goes haywire, we live in a small town."

"Right," I said, feeling the sting of rejection down to my toes. I inched out of the bed. I'd just crawl away to my room. I'd stay there until our flight left in a few days.

"Where the hell are you going?" he demanded.

"Um . . . back to my room."

"What the fuck? Why?"

"You just said . . . small town."

"Listen, country boy. You wanna give this a shot or don't you?"

I opened my mouth to speak, but somebody was fumbling with keys at the front door of the bungalow.

"Can you believe it?" he asked.

We poked our heads outside the bedroom door. A trio of maids rolled in fresh fruit, more champagne and fresh linens.

"Let's go for a swim." Nelson grinned at me. "Let's cool off and come back and if we still want to do this, we'll do it."

I didn't argue, though I doubted a swim would cool me

off any.

We donned shorts and walked down to the beach. The morning bloomed, sunny and hot. We reached the ocean and saw a guy kite surfing in the distance.

"I'd love to try that some time," Nelson said. He looked so handsome, his face the most amazing one I'd ever seen. I felt every shadow of doubt, every smudge of hurt in the beauty of his eyes.

"Can I kiss you?" I asked.

"God, yes."

I leaned in and tasted his lips. I liked the way he kissed me back. I loved his hard, muscular body. Damn. I wished we were alone some place.

His arms moved around me.

When he pulled me in tight, I felt his hard cock jabbing at my belly. I got more than a small thrill that I could excite him this way. I smiled against his kiss. He smiled right back.

"It feels nice, doesn't it?" he asked.

Wow. It felt incredible. I moved in for a kiss when I heard Quinn's mad laughter behind us. Oh, shit.

"Hey," Rex said, coming down the rocky path toward us. "You two look cozy."

"Yeah," I said. I felt my insecurities pile up like a slow jam on the 405 freeway. He was gonna swoop in and drag Nelson off to his lair again. Nelson however, stayed where he was. I noticed Rex's look of astonishment. Up until now, every time we'd seen them, Nelson had been more than happy to see him.

"You going for a swim?" he asked.

"Yep," I said. I glanced at Quinn. I stared hard. He'd gone and shaved his head and had the same goofy tattoo on his neck. What the hell was going on?

"We should get back," Nelson said. "We're meeting friends. Have a great swim."

"Toodles," Quinn said. His smile was forced and bright.

"Friends?" I hissed as soon I thought we were out of ear-shot. "What friends?"

"I had to say something. Quinn's all upset that Rex has pretty much ignored him since they got here. Last night, he was upset and so was I. He thought I wanted Rex. I'm actually more attracted to Quinn and, to be honest, more attracted to you than either of them."

"You are?" I felt myself glowing with happiness.

"Haven't I been trying to tell you that?"

I shrugged. "It's nice to hear it."

He grinned. "You've come a long way in twenty-four hours."

"I was so jealous and mad when I saw you with Rex."

"That was just sex and, to be honest . . . it wasn't that good. He's such a numbers queen. No heart. Quinn is a sweet guy who could do a lot better."

"You really like him, huh?"

"Not the way I like you. Hey, Jimmy taught me a word that fits exactly what I think of you."

"Yeah, what's that?"

"Swaggerific. Isn't that a great word?"

"I'm swaggerific?"

"Zeen. That means oh, yes."

I caught his hand in mine. His warm fingers threaded against my own. I felt my cock hardening in my shorts. It had been a long time since I felt this kind of sexual heat.

We hurried to the bungalow. The magic room fairies had disappeared, leaving the place looking and smelling like fresh, fragrant flowers.

"Your room or mine?" Nelson asked, his voice husky.

"Mine," I said. "I tried your bed out last night."

He laughed as I grabbed his hand and dragged him in there.

"You should have stopped me going into Rex's room with him last night," he said as we stood facing one another.

"I was afraid of making an ass of myself."

His fingers trailed across my face and throat. He took my face in his hands and kissed me. We picked up exactly where we'd left off down at the beach. It still made my cock go hard and my sexual quandaries fly out the window. We took each other's clothes off. I let my fingers linger against his hard, lean body. I kissed him and kept thinking about the drink Jimmy had given me. The slippery nipple. For some reason, it made me think of Nelson's nipple and I wanted to taste it. I dipped down and took his left nipple into my mouth. His cock flipped up to me. He let out a gasp, his hands moving to my head. I suckled, enjoying his body's responses. He took it away from me and fed me the right nipple, too.

I kissed him again, my hand finally moving to his cock.

"Nelson, you have to teach me. Show me how to make you feel good."

"Okay," he said.

We pulled back the bed covers and slipped between the cool, crisp sheets together. I had a sudden flash of making love to him, of being immersed inside him. I wanted that. Lord, I wanted *him*.

"Like this." He took hold of my cock. "There are two schools of thought about blowjobs but I personally love sucking a man off. Some people think it isn't safe. How about you?"

"No. I want to do it with you. We can fuck with condoms though."

"Look at you. All confident about fucking." He grinned when he said this. His fingers roamed my cock, and he enticed some insta-lust the likes of which I had never experienced dead sober before. I wanted to suck him, too, but he wanted to bring me off. We argued about it until I won by licking his cock head. He suddenly stopped all his bossy talk.

"Oh, fuck," he said.

I scooted down and held him the way he'd taught me. His cock was huge but nowhere near the lethal weapon I'd seen on Jimmy. I loved the taste and texture of him. I'd tasted my own come before but nothing tasted like this. Nelson tasted gorgeous. He was salty, sweet, manly and juicy at the same time. I gently moved his hips to get more of him in my mouth. I breathed through my nose. I didn't gag and he didn't push too hard. I focused on not grazing his beautiful shaft with my teeth. I didn't want to do anything at all that could hurt this man. I felt his trust, his desire, and I felt it all back for him. In spades.

Fuck, he tasted amazing.

When he came, I was shocked how hard he burst inside my mouth. He fucked against me, calling my name, his fingers clutching my head.

Then it was my turn. He gave as good as he got, his fingers gently holding my balls. It felt better than Jimmy's tugging. I realized I had feelings for Nelson. That was why it felt so good. He brought me to a roaring orgasm, his fingers strolling along my ass crack.

I collapsed back on the bed. He scooted up and kissed me.

We couldn't keep our hands off each other. We kept swapping kisses, our cocks hard again.

"How do you feel about fucking me?" he asked.

"It's . . . wow, it's all I can think about."

"If you fuck me, you have to prepare me."

"You mean, suck your ass?"

He nodded.

"I want to." I wanted to lay claim to his ass. Jealousy gripped me. "Did Rex fuck you?"

His cheeks reddened. "Yes. Once. He tried again last night but he was too stoned."

"Good. I never want him to fuck you again."

Nelson smiled at me. "You are full of surprises today, Johnny."

He kissed me, and I lay beside him, my hands luxuriating in the feel of him. When my hand got to his balls, he opened his legs. I thought it would be difficult. I was surprised when I got down there how clean and manly he smelled. I couldn't wait to lick him. I pressed kisses and licks along the sensitive skin between his balls and ass. I toyed with his ball sac the way Jimmy had with me. It seemed to send Nelson into orbit. His legs opened wider, and my mouth sucked harder. His body seemed to open to me. He pulled on his cock, holding his balls away from me to give me better access to his hole. I kissed and licked his balls, squeezed between his fingers.

Man, I wanted to fuck him badly.

"Where are your rubbers?" he asked.

I got off the bed. I hated leaving him even for a minute. When I got back on the bed, he sat up, reaching for my cock. He sucked on me, as I eased him down to the bed. I wanted to suck him off again but he wanted to come with my cock inside him. I rolled on a condom.

Poised between his legs, I loved the smile he gave me.

"I've wanted this for so long," he said.

"You have?"

He nodded. "Billy encouraged me to invite you on this trip."

"Holy shit. Everybody in the world knew I was gay before I did?"

He laughed, his fingers moving to my face. He pushed back tendrils of damp hair from my eyes. I hadn't realized I'd worked up such a sweat.

"Hurry up and fuck me," he said.

"Yessir."

I rubbed my sheathed cock against his ass.

"Lube?" he asked.

I stared down at him.

"Darling, I'm not a girl. They get wet down there. I'm a boy. As much as you excite me, I need a little help. Stay right there."

He ran off to his bedroom and came back with little foil packs.

"More rubbers?" I asked.

"Not that we won't need 'em, but no. They're travel packs of lube."

"I guess I'm not that gay after all."

He laughed. "You're a fresh fish. My favorite kind."

Nelson and I began the kissing, sucking, licking thing again and it didn't take long to get us both back into the groove. I would have taken my time entering him, but man oh man he was ready and needy. He gripped my ass. He felt so fucking hot and wonderful. Being inside him was totally different from being in a woman. It felt right. It felt good. The fire of hope, of life, spiraled through me.

"Oh, fuck me, Johnny."

His cock lay between our mashing bodies. I looked down, amazed at how beautiful it looked. Yeah, I wanted to come inside him, deep, hard and blissfully, but I wanted him to come even more. I balanced myself on my knees, on one el-bow, one hand reaching between us so I could hold him when he came. His whole face changed. He babbled insensi-bly but I understood every heated word. We came together, and I fucked him more and more. His legs wrapped around me.

I'd never fucked anyone like this in my life. His hands left my ass cheeks and wound around my neck. I touched his forehead with my lips, his pulse beating erratically. He was so fucking hot I couldn't believe it.

Nelson and I stayed like this for long minutes. I hated pulling out of him.

"Well?" he asked when I rolled off him. He lay on one elbow, close to me, looking into my face.

"I can't believe it," I said.

"And you know what?"

"What?" I felt a swirl of emotions, all of them good.

"It's only going to get better."

"Is that possible."

He gave me that brilliant smile. The one I'd come to think of as the smile just for me.

"Yes, sweetheart. You'll see."

His hands stroked my face and neck, his feverish lips closing on mine. When he finished giving me the most ardent tongue kiss I'd ever experienced, we took deep, gulping breaths.

"Do we have to leave this room?" I asked.

"Not unless we want to. I'm thinking a moonlight swim."

I glanced at him. He put his hand on my cheek.

"Just the two of us, Johnny."

I nodded. I liked the idea of that.

"Will you excuse me a moment?"

"Sure," he said. He watched me going over to the computer. It was still turned on. "I have to send Ellis an email.

My new sweetheart lay on the bed, looking amazing and edible. It was hard to tear my gaze from him. I typed fast.

Bad news.

Ellis emailed back: *What??*

How attached are you to the ten dollars you bet Gen?

A pause, then: *What??*

Sorry to tell you, but I think I'm gay. I also think I'm in love. See you in a few days.

He wrote back: *I knew I'd lose that bet.* :)

I turned around and caught Nelson standing beside me, looking over my shoulder.

"You think you're in love?" he asked. "You only *think*?"

I leaned into him, burying my face in his hard belly. He smelled of sun, sex and . . . me.

"Forgive me, Nelson. It's all so new."

"Hey, country boy." His voice softened as he stroked my head. "Come to bed and show me how you feel."

I looked up at him. "No more porn stars?"

He gazed down at me, that brilliant smile reaching places in my heart I never knew existed before.

"What porn stars? There's nobody for me but you."

I pushed him back onto the bed. Our hard cocks collided, and our mouths met in a hard kiss. My email inbox beeped. I didn't care. Nelson wanted me and I wanted him. Like I'd never, ever wanted anyone before in my life.

I leaned down and touched his feet. I wanted to kiss him from the ground up.

"Thank God," he whispered, pulling me up to his face. "Thank God you're gay."

I covered his body with my own. Yeah. Thank God I was. I kissed his face until I made him laugh, his insistent cock grazing my thigh. So many places on his body to kiss. But where to start? I went back to his toes. We had time. All the time in the world.

That thought was Zeen. And totally swaggerific.

About the Author

J.C. Raefael writes the kind of stories she loves to read herself. Life in her hometown of Ojai, California, might be slow, but orange groves and cowboys are a strong part of life. She dreams of a Mardi Gras taking place on Ojai Avenue with drag queens, a gay parade Marshal and colorful floats. Oh, well, she is safe to dream.

Contact her at jcraefael@gmail.com

www.ingramcontent.com/pod-product-compliance
Lightning Source LLC
Chambersburg PA
CBHW070536130626
46555CB00003B/1449